For fourteen years now *Perry Rhodan* has been acknowledged to be the world's top-selling science fiction series. Originally published in magazine form in Germany, the series has now appeared in hardback and paperback in the States.

Over five hundred *Perry Rhodan* clubs exist on the Continent and *Perry Rhodan* fan conventions are held annually. The first *Perry Rhodan* film, *SOS From Outer Space,* has now been released in Europe.

The series has sold over 150 million copies in Europe alone.

D1353321

Also available in the *Perry Rhodan* series

Clark Darlton

Perry Rhodan 15
Escape to Venus

Futura Publications Limited
An Orbit Book

An Orbit Book

First published in Great Britain in 1976
by Futura Publications Limited

Copyright © Ace Books 1972

An Ace Book, by arrangement with Arthur Moewig
Verlag
This series was created by Karl-Herbert Scheer and
Walter Ernsting, translated by Wendayne Ackerman
and edited by Forrest J. Ackerman and Frederik Pohl

ISBN: 0 8600 7895 7

This English edition dedicated to Edgar Rice
Burroughs Whose 'Escape On Venus' Was Just One
Of His Myriads Of Marvellous Classics Of Escape
Literature

Printed in Great Britain by
Hazell Watson & Viney Ltd
Aylesbury, Bucks

Futura Publications Limited
110 Warner Road
Camberwell, London SE5

HELL WORLD

Three metal monsters.

Three silvery, glittering bodies of metal reared up from the soil of Asia towards the eternally blue sky of the great continent. Their conical noses seemed to sniff toward the stars.

On the exterior, the spaceships resembled the first rockets that flew from the Earth to the Moon, initiating a new era for mankind. But the resemblance was strictly external.

Internally, the ships were equipped with far ranging ray cannons and machines to throw up energy screens around them, protective barriers impenetrable by any power on Earth. These were the latest type of 'destroyers,' craft built on an enlarged scale with a complement of three men and capable of light speed.

Constructed in the space complex of the New Power, the three destroyers were the first of their kind and so far had been test flown only once. No defects or malfunctions had been discovered so mass production of the new model was scheduled for the near future in the largest spaceship construction center in the world.

Lonely lay the spacious test terrain of the New Power under the broiling heat of the afternoon sun. In the distance soared the skyscrapers of Terrania, formerly known as Galacto-City, the future capital of a united world. To the left was the spacecraft plant, a vast complex of long halls, immense hangars and a variety of domed buildings.

Guards patrolled the immediate area around the three new destroyers. Mechanically, and at regular intervals, they performed their duties, looking neither to right nor to left, as if they realized how senseless their task must be: for no one could possibly advance undetected to this point. No unauthorized person was to be found anywhere throughout the entire area of the plant – the electronically controlled cordon saw to that.

The guards did not wear uniforms; instead, garments of a strange-looking metallic material that shone like silver in the sun. Their ever alert eyes were not organic, they were crystal lenses. For these were no ordinary human beings: they were robots.

Theirs was a single command: to guard the ships. This they did without emotion. When ordered to watch for some one who could not possibly appear here, no one could have told whether there was any sensation of amazement or not in their positronic brains.

To the right, as far as the horizon, extended the mirror-like expanse of the Goshun saltlake. From this side there was the least potential threat of intruders for the lake lay within the cordonned-off area.

And still, this calm was deceptive.

While all mankind was preparing to celebrate an important anniversary of man's first flight to the Moon, and hardly a soul was not glued to TV to watch the festivities, one person had decided to no longer place faith in certain promises. The time had come for action!

A car was approaching the test area from the south.

The smooth road was almost free of dust. The vehicle whizzed along the deserted road, never slowing down, not even when the first electronic barrier came into sight. The electronic sensors checked out the vehicle and its occupants – and let them pass.

The second and third electronic checkpoints reacted in a similar manner.

The car, a smart-looking sports model, drove straight toward the three rockets and then began to decrease its

6

speed. Two of the robot guards had changed the course of their mechanical rounds and advanced toward the car. Their left arms were held at a strange angle but nobody could have recognized the rayguns hidden inside. The least impulse would be sufficient to transform these apparently harmless metal creatures into energy-spewing death-dealing machines.

But that impulse failed to materialize.

The electronic sensors probed the brain pattern of the human being that had stepped out of the vehicle and it was checked out as 'approved,' as it possessed all the necessary required qualifications. The two robots lowered their arms and permitted the person to pass. With a sarcastic smile, the stranger walked past the automatons, then stopped a few yards farther away, seemingly undecided.

There they were, the three small model spaceships, ready to start. Their height of 30 yards made them appear quite huge, judged by terrestrial standards. Their interior harbored tremendous energy reservoirs and fantastic engines designed by non-human brains. With these ships it was possible to traverse the solar system within the span of a few hours and, if one so desired, one could reach the nearest star in $4\frac{1}{2}$ years.

The robots resumed their interrupted patrols. The stranger's brain pattern spelt no danger, according to their programmed instructions, so the unidentified one was permitted to pass; indeed, allowed to do much more without releasing danger impulses in their positronic brains.

The tall stranger stood for quite a while in the solitude of the desert and contemplated the three spacecraft. The well-fitting uniform brought out the stranger's slender figure and at closer examination it became evident that this was a *female* figure. A big cap hid the long, light-colored hair that shone almost white in the bright sun. The reddish eyes revealed determination – as well as a trace of sadness.

The woman threw a last glance at everything around her – the nearby salt lake, the vast aircraft plant and the distant city of Terrania – before she slowly started to move in the direction of the nearest of the three spaceships.

It was the third destroyer C, or D3 for short.

The entrance hatch of D3 was closed but there was a small metal ladder leading up to it. One of the robots was standing at the foot of this ladder. He did not move as the woman came closer and then stopped in front of him. The robot's left arm hung down his side without moving. There was a blank stare in his crystal lenses.

'Proceed to your station, R-17,' said the woman in a harsh-sounding unknown language after she had quickly read the robot's name on a small sign on his chest. 'We are starting a test flight.'

The robot remained motionless. 'There is no command for such a test flight,' he answered in the same language.

The woman reacted with a gesture of displeasure. 'I am issuing the command now, I, Thora of Arkon.'

R-17 still did not react in the desired manner. 'Rhodan's order supercedes yours, Thora.'

Angry sparks glittered in the woman's eyes. Fiery flashes seemed to dart from her red pupils toward the resistant robot.

'Perry Rhodan is a Terranian, R-17, and I am an Arkonide. My command is higher than that of Rhodan, the earthling.'

'Also higher than that of Khrest?'

She hesitated for a moment, then threw her head back indignantly. 'Khrest is under Rhodan's influence – he doesn't count any longer. Why are you asking?'

'Because Khrest has ordered that we should obey all commands coming from Rhodan whatever they might be.

Therefore we cannot act *against* his orders. That is logical, isn't it?'

The woman thought for a moment, then slowly nodded her head. 'Yes, that sounds quite logical. Do you always react according to logical principles, R-17?'

'My existence is based on logic.'

'Good,' said the woman and regarded his almost human features with a pensive expression in her eyes. 'Then will you answer some questions I have?'

'With pleasure, Thora of Arkon.'

'Did Perry Rhodan specifically forbid another test flight with D3?'

'No.'

'Furthermore, has he forbidden that I undertake such a test flight?'

'No.'

'Would you therefore be acting against Rhodan's orders if you were to fly this ship to Venus, for instance?'

'Conditionally it seems: No.'

'Well, then,' Thora breathed a sigh of relief. 'It follows that you are not breaking any rules if you do as I say.'

R-17's features almost seemed to express some doubt. 'But I did not receive any orders from Rhodan for this flight.'

'Is that necessary?' Thora appeared very astonished. 'After all you are receiving such an order from myself now. And you were not forbidden to receive orders from me – or am I wrong?'

'No.'

Thora smiled. Her smile had no effect on the robot's psycho-regions, only the compelling logic of her question affected him.

'No, it is not forbidden to receive any orders from you.'

'Alright, we can start then!'

R-17 was still hesitating. As far as it was possible for

9

him at all, he did not seem to feel too happy with his existence. But he could not find any logical counter argument to blankly refuse Thora's request. This woman was a member of the race that had created him, while Rhodan was merely an inhabitant of this planet by the name of Terra – although he was a particularly outstanding specimen of that race. Thora was much closer to R-17 than Rhodan, although he had been forced to obey him as a result of conditioning received at the hands of Khrest. He would never disregard this command to obey him. He would be incapable of doing so without bringing about a disastrous short circuit in his system.

On the other hand, if he were to obey Thora he would not act directly against Rhodan's orders; ergo, he was not exposing himself to any danger.

He nodded his head in a human-like gesture. 'Yes, we can start. My orders were not to permit any strangers to approach this ship. Thora of Arkon, however, is no stranger.'

'Fine. Let's not waste any time. Set course for the planet Venus as fast as you can manage. I want to test how fast we can reach our second base in this solar system in case of emergency.'

She was waiting impatiently as the robot rather clumsily climbed up the ladder and opened the entrance hatch. Not until he had disappeared in the airlock did she follow him up into the ship. The robot pushed a button and the heavy outside hatch fell shut. The anti-grav elevator brought Thora and R-17 within a few seconds up to the destroyer's nose, where the command center was located.

They sat down in the movable seats. While the robot was calculating the course, the engines began to warm up. Somewhere in the interior of D3 the reactor began to work, producing the incredible amounts of energy needed to lift the ship off the ground against the gravitational pull, then hurtle it through space with the speed of light. The artificial grav-fields were switched on automatically to neutralize any G-forces. The entire complicated mechanism of an unimaginable technology was set in motion.

Thora was waiting. She knew she had accomplished her aim. It would be just a few more minutes, then she would watch this hated planet sink away like a blue sphere in the ocean of infinity. Venus would be only a stopover, for it would be sheer madness to try reaching her home planet, more than 30-thousand light-years away, with a ship limited to the speed of light. But on Venus there was a hyperwave sender and it would certainly not be too difficult to call one of the Arkonide space cruisers to come to her rescue.

R-17 motioned to her. 'All ready for take-off. Observe the videoscreen to acquaint yourself with the capacities of D3. Rhodan has strictly forbidden maximum speed; this is permitted only in case of an emergency. Still, we'll reach Venus in about one hour and a half. Venus is now on the other side of the sun.'

'Distance?'

R-17 answered immediately: '143 million miles.'

'Our top permissible speed?'

'75% that of light.'

She did not reply and waited. R-17 seized a lever and pulled it downwards. Nothing seemed to happen but the image on the videoscreen underwent rapid changes.

D3 lifted off without using the pulse-drive power unit. The antigrav projectors nullified the gravitational pull of Earth, and repelling force-fields moved the now weightless mass of the spaceship.

The ground fell away suddenly from underneath the ship. Buildings, roads, rivers, mountains and deserts seemed to fly rapidly and evenly from all sides toward the center of the starting point, and the field of vision expanded until the entire terrain suddenly dropped away and was replaced by a dark-violet area.

The universe!

In less than 10 seconds the destroyer had rammed through Earth's atmosphere and was now unrelentingly racing through space.

For a moment, Thora thought she recognized a flashing point in the right corner of the observation screen; but almost before she became consciously aware of it, the light point had disappeared again. Then she noticed the sun, nearly straight ahead in the rocket's line of flight, its brightness considerably reduced by dark filters.

Earth assumed the shape of a globe that rotated peacefully in the starry sky, becoming smaller and smaller until it was nothing but a brightly shining heavenly body.

Thora sighed. She glanced in the direction of the robot pilot.

R-17 returned her glance. 'A fine ship,' he said with appreciation.

'True, a fine ship, but not good enough for what I have in mind, R-17.'

The robot did not ask any questions. Silently he set the course, made adjustments and calculated.

The sun seemed to be threateningly close.

For quite some time the manned space station had been revolving around the Earth. Together with two other space stations, it maintained a worldwide television network. The three stations were circling at the exact altitude where the speed of their orbit equalled that of Earth's rotation, in this manner constantly over the same spot on the world's surface.

Radio operator Adams was fully aware of his responsibility as he established communication with the two other stations in order to begin the broadcast of 'Terra-Television.'

It was 10 years to the day since the venture into space had started under the command of the then totally unknown Major Perry Rhodan. The *Stardust* had landed on the Moon, found there the wrecked remnants of an Arkonide space expedition whose female commander Thora together with the leading scientist Khrest accompanied the successful space mission back to Earth. This had been the beginning of a new era, reflected Adams.

Station II confirmed establishment of contact and within a few seconds the other space station followed suit. Adams now called Earth. The big broadcast center in Terrania answered. Now the worldwide broadcast could begin.

Radio operator Adams leaned back comfortably in his chair. There was not much more for him to do; the rest would follow automatically. Still, he wanted to make sure he didn't miss this historic occasion. Perry Rhodan in person was scheduled to address mankind.

On the monitor a whirling star cluster appeared which soon changed into the familiar picture of the Milky Way, slowly rotating against the dark background of infinity. This was the TV identification of Terrania, the capital of the New Power.

Now the face of a man appeared on the monitor screen. It was a lean well-cut face. Its deep lines, especially around the mouth, made the man look older than he actually might be.

'This is Colonel Michael Freyt speaking from Terrania. On the occasion of our 10th national space holiday, I present to you Perry Rhodan, president of the New Power and friend of the Arkonides.'

The man's image vanished from the screen and was replaced by another face. A clicking noise could be heard as the simultan-translator installations were switched on.

Perry Rhodan's words would be translated into all languages of the world as quickly as spoken.

How strange, thought Adams, this similarity between Freyt's and Rhodan's features. They might almost be mistaken for brothers. The same lean figure, the same steel-gray eyes and the sharp lines around nose and mouth. Even the identical, purposeful glance! But Rhodan is the younger of the two – or could I be mistaken? He ought to be more than 45 by now, still he doesn't look a day over 38. Sure would like to know how he manages to keep young like that! That uniform suits him to a T. Must be about 10 years since he exchanged the uniform of an American test pilot for it. What a wild story that was way back. . . .

But fortunately, Adams had to miss the beginning of Rhodan's speech. The shrill sound of an alarm bell rang throughout the space station and startled him from his reminiscing. He jumped up and rushed to the door.

An alarm signal on the space station always meant danger.

But they were lucky this time. The man on guard duty had observed an unidentified flying object on the radar screen. This UFO had raced close by the station with tremendous speed and had disappeared in the direction of the Moon. Evidently it had come from Earth.

'From Earth?' wondered Adams. He sounded very doubtful. 'Have you checked this out with Terrania?'

'Not yet.'

'Get it! Pronto, old man!' recommended Adams and comforted himself with the thought that the most interesting talks usually start out with boring introductory remarks. He would probably not miss too much if he would first wait for the answer from Terrania.

Terrania reported almost immediately: 'No spaceship has taken off from here. We need further data from you.'

14

Further data! That was a tall order! The spaceship, assuming even that the UFO had been a spaceship, had whizzed by so incredibly fast that very little had been observed about it. Perhaps the continuously running film camera might supply some more information. The film had just emerged from the developer.

The picture showed a ship about 30-yards long with a rather narrow diameter. Something like a torpedo. Velocity: could not be exactly determined but certainly in excess of 60 miles/sec^2.

Adams shook his head as he heard his colleagues send these data back to the control station on Earth. Assuming that such a ship really did exist, then it must have come from Perry Rhodan's secret aircraft installations about which so little was known. Unless one believed the rumors . . .

The answer from Terrania came surprisingly quick and it was not what Adams had expected:

'Try at once to obtain further data from our station on the Moon. Important to get a report on the presumed course of the unknown ship. We are also interested to learn more about the ship's velocity when passing in the vicinity of the Moon. Thanks for your help. We are awaiting further reports from you. Meanwhile we will also investigate from this end.'

That was all. The radar observer glanced at Adams.

'Well, what do you say to that? Sounds funny, doesn't it?'

'Anything that has to do with Rhodan is strange,' replied Adams. 'I wonder if that ship has taken off without their consent down there in Terrania.'

He turned away and walked back to his own work station without paying any further attention to his colleague's dumbfounded face.

Adams arrived back just in time to hear Perry Rhodan

say on the videoscreen: '. . . established with the help of the Arkonides a third power, the New Power, which thus far has always been successful in settling all conflicts between the other two power blocs of the world. As a result of the events in the past year, we no longer can consider the Eastern Bloc as one of the world powers, and must expect it to be annexed sooner or later by the Asiatic Federation. Since, however, the AF is on good political terms with the Western Bloc, the ideal of one united government of the world is coming closer to realization.

'All of you, my fellow Earthmen, are aware of the fact that a Federal Government of the World is one of my political goals. Ever since the time when the Arkonides were shipwrecked on the Moon, helpless despite their tremendous technological means and therefore dependent on mankind's coming to their rescue, they have been our allies. This gave me the power potential to establish a united world government by *force*. However, I consider such methods to be wrong. Such an ideal world government must evolve *organically* and out of mankind's own *free will* – and I assure you that this will come about in due time. Just as the various nations had to abandon their petty pride and join either the Western or the Eastern Federation, so also the two big power blocs will have to realize some day that only one United Earth can assume its historical role within the Galaxy.

'Much has been accomplished within the past 10 years. Thanks to the technological help we received from our Arkonide friends (who are the rulers of a gigantic star realm, more than 30,000 light-years distant from here) we have succeeded in building a space fleet for the New Power, capable of defending our planet against extraterrestrial attacks. We have already established good trade relations with one of the races living far away on other planets in the universe. We were also fortunate in warding off an invasion of a hostile non-human race. We built the most modern metropolis of the world in the barren Gobi desert: Terrania, formerly known as Galacto-City. All this combined has lifted our old world out of its former isolation. It now has become a power factor that even the Arkonides cannot ignore – once they discover our planet.

'And this brings me to a point that I want to discuss here quite frankly before all of you, my listeners. There are only two Arkonides who know that our world exists: Khrest, the former scientific leader of the space exploratory mission we found stranded on our moon, and which by now must be assumed to be lost without a trace by their own people on their home planet Arkon – and the female commander of that expedition, Thora. So far I have always managed to prevent these two Arkonides from establishing communication with their own world. I did this for a very simple reason: if ever the people of Arkon should discover the existence of our Earth, they would be most interested to incorporate our world into their galactic empire, for as far as they are concerned we are a backward race, in need of their superior political and technological support.

'Khrest and Thora promised to wait for their return to Arkon till Earth would be ready to properly receive a visit of the Arkonide race. But this can only take place when the Arkonide delegation will be met by a strong and united Earth. Earth cannot be truly united until we have a world government. You will therefore appreciate my endeavors towards the solution of this particular problem.

'For quite a number of years now the New Power has been preparing for the establishment of a united government of all mankind. Some day we will put at the disposal of all the nations of this planet our Arkonide technology which surpasses the wildest imagination. I founded the General Cosmic Company, which undoubtedly has become the most significant economic power factor of the world.

17

My company, the GCC, controls the production and the economy of Earth, if I may say so. We determine the monetary standards. And, quite logically, one day the GCC will introduce the future Terranian currency – we have the means to do so.

'Now it is exclusively up to you and to your respective governments as to when all of this will become a reality. But this day must come soon. I want to emphasize again that I will avoid using force, even if it were child's play for me, to forge ahead with my plans for such a Federated World Government.

'But I cannot postpone this too much longer. For the very simple reason that Khrest and Thora are urging me to let them return to their planet home. I cannot much longer deny them this very justified request, for I, as well as all the rest of mankind, are in deep debt to these two Arkonides. Without their help we would still be standing at the threshold of space travel and would have to be satisfied if just now we were starting to send the first rockets to Venus. Therefore, you have only a short time at your disposal in which to bring about an agreement amongst yourselves. Then, as soon as the new united world government has been established, we shall be ready to meet the Arkonides – and with this the challenge of an entire galactic empire.

'Let me describe, now, how I envision such a world government . . .'

Radio operator Adams stretched out his long legs. He was not too much interested in listening to further details about this plan of a world government. True, the idea was not bad, but what the politicians of the two power blocs would have to say to it was something else again. It had become quite evident when the Eastern Bloc rebelled that time against Rhodan, how little it had pleased them to have to acknowledge the technological superiority of the New

18

Power. All this had ended, temporarily maybe, when the army of the Eastern Bloc had suffered a decisive defeat on Venus. The Eastern armed forces had landed on the second planet from the sun and had lost their way in the swamps and jungles of this primeval world. The armies were missing and had not been heard of since. Rhodan's base on Venus, however, had automatically repelled any attack with the use of positronically guided weapons.

Adams sighed. Maybe his colleague had some more news by now about the mysterious spaceship. He listened for another moment to Rhodan's broadcast and learned how Rhodan planned to have the projected world government share in his existing space fighter fleet. Adams got up and went to the radar center.

He arrived just at the right moment.

The monitor screen, connecting the space station with Terrania, showed the excited face of a heavy-built man who seemed to be gasping for air. Just like a fish on dry land, noted Adams. Then he tried to remember where he had seen that face before. Blast it, wasn't that Reginald Bell, Rhodan's friend and constant companion, who had become the Minister of Security Forces of the New Power?

He examined the face closer as he shut the door behind him. The videoscreen presented a true-to-life three-dimensional color picture of that furious face.

'Will you get a move on, slowpoke!' panted Bell, enraged. 'I need to know the course of that ship you observed a little while ago. Didn't you get a reply from the moon station, huh?'

'Just got it,' growled Adams' colleague and pulled over a slip of paper and looked at it. 'What's all the fuss about? Wasn't that ship supposed to take off?'

'Mind your own business! You'll find out soon enough. Let me have the data, will you, please? Hurry up!'

'The ship was located by the direction finders of our

19

lunar installations – although its speed was quite considerable already. No course change could be determined. The ship was flying almost straight toward the sun.'

'Toward the sun?' gasped the man visible on the videoscreen: Reginald Bell. 'What does this crazy woman want on or in the sun?'

'Who?' asked the radar operator.

Bell waved him off with an impatient movement of his hand. 'Let her roast there for all I care. Hope that'll make her a bit more palatable and melt that cold chunk of ice! The sun!'

The radar operator grinned. 'May I remind you,' he said, 'that there is not only the sun between here and the direction toward the sun.'

'What do you mean by that?' Bell asked, puzzled. But he had hardly finished speaking when he suddenly turned pale. His ruddy complexion miraculously changed to a muddy gray. 'Not only the sun . . . ? Damn it, you're right! Why didn't you say so right away? Thanks for the information – I'll show my appreciation some time.'

'Just tell me what's going on down there!' begged the radar operator, but the screen had gone dark again. This was Bell's own way of getting out of giving an answer.

Adams shrugged his shoulders. 'Don't worry about it, John. Reginald Bell is supposed to be quite an odd bird, they say.'

The radar operator did not react to his friend's remark. 'I wonder what kind of a ship that was we saw? Seems to have caused quite a ruckus when it took off.'

'Not the ship, I think.' Adams spoke in enigmatic tones. 'I believe it must have been the *woman* Bell mentioned who caused all the commotion. No wonder; after all, the ship took off from the Gobi Desert.'

'If I only had some idea what it's all about,' commented

the radar operator, 'I could make a fortune. I have some connections with a newspaper reporter . . .'

Adams frowned and returned to his own section. The broadcast was still going on and once more he reclined comfortably in his armchair.

Perry Rhodan was still talking.

'. . . are we living today no longer have the mistaken notion that we are the only intelligent life in this universe. We are not alone; quite the contrary. We are in the same situation as the inhabitants of an isolated island in the Pacific Ocean who up to this moment believed themselves to be the only living men on this world and suddenly find out that they are surrounded – better, locked in – by huge continents with millions of human beings. What would make more sense for the islanders than to join together, forget their petty squabbles and face the unknown as one united force?'

Perry Rhodan paused.

None of the Earth viewers of this telecast noticed this slight intermission for nobody speaks without an occasional break. But Adams was not on Earth, he was on space station III. And besides, he knew about the mysterious ship that had so excited the Minister of Security of the New Power. And in addition he knew that Rhodan had under his command a mutant corps with some excellent telepaths.

Lastly, Adams had a great talent for putting two and two together.

It was not feasible, he thought, to call Perry Rhodan away from the TV cameras in the middle of an address to a worldwide audience. Yet he had to be informed if something important happened during it. And that this event had been quite important had been fully evidenced by Reginald Bell's behavior.

Therefore . . .

No, it was truly not difficult for radio operator Adams to understand the meaning of what was taking place now on the videoscreen right in front of his eyes.

Perry Rhodan fell silent and seemed to ponder something for a moment. He gazed at some imaginary point and slightly narrowed his eyes. He seemed to listen to some voice that spoke to him from a spot invisible to his audience. A deep furrow appeared in his brow. For an instant his eyes flashed with displeasure but then his friendly open smile returned. He looked once more straight into the camera, directly into the eyes of the whole world. His voice had not changed at all as he resumed his talk:

'But many problems still remain to be solved and I must ask you to continue to have confidence in me. And, please, keep trusting our two Arkonide friends regardless of what might happen. If ever one of them should decide to communicate with Arkon and one of the many belligerent races of the universe should learn – if only by accident – of the existence of Earth, the danger of our being discovered would increase tremendously. And you know as well as I what the result would be if mankind were not united by then.

'In this connection I would like to remind you that we are celebrating here not only the anniversary of man's conquest of space but at the same time the final establishment of peace. The New Power loves peace but will hit swift and hard, should peace be disturbed anywhere in this world.'

After this somewhat abrupt conclusion of his speech, Rhodan bowed slightly in the direction of his invisible audience and walked quickly to a door through which he disappeared. For some time this door could still be seen on the videoscreen, before Col Freyt appeared to announce that Reginald Bell, the Minister of Security of the New

Power, would shortly speak about problems of defense in case of an invasion by hostile aliens.

Freyt asked the listeners to be patient for a while, since Bell had been detained by some unforseen difficulties.

Radio operator Adams decided to wait. He had the feeling he had witnessed some important events that could have long lasting effects.

The sun had become a glowing ball of gas that quickly passed by to the left of the spaceship. Giant protuberances shot out into the void and seemed to want to pull in the destroyer C with fiery fingers, but the ship was too fast. It raced past the sun at half the speed of light and could no longer be overtaken by the whirling gas masses.

Robot R-17 sat motionless in front of the controls which he had mainly switched over to the automatic guidance system. Only occasionally would he carry out a slight course correction which had become necessary because of the mighty gravitational pull of the sun. He remained silent, waiting for further events.

Thora had ordered him to name her the commander of this destroyer when they were passing near the moon base. But before the station could reply they had long since vanished in the darkness of space.

This time she was determined not to permit anything to interfere with her plans. For 10 years – if one took into consideration the peculiar time-leap on Wanderer, the planet of eternal life – she had submitted to Rhodan's iron will. But now she realized he had not the slightest intention of permitting her and Khrest to return to Arkon.

First, he had said, he wanted to organize his terrestrial world government, not lose face before the Arkonides. Of course, he always used the cheap pretext that an invasion was forever threatening his race.

Very well then, if Rhodan would not give her permission she would simply take what was her due right. On Venus she would find a way to provide herself with a ship which could carry her back to her home planet. All she needed was to reach the hypersender on Venus that would carry her words with faster-than-light speed through the emptiness of space to distant Arkon.

Her compatriots would send a ship to rescue her and thus her imprisonment would end.

She had reached this point in her deliberations when she was seized by some doubts. She had failed to inform Khrest of her plan although he was entitled to know about it. But Khrest was on Rhodan's side; he would not understand her. Therefore she had to proceed without him.

Nevertheless . . .

Seconds turned into minutes. Long since the sun had shrunk in size behind the rear of her ship although it still looked much larger than when seen from Earth. Now a brightly shining point detached itself from the crowded cluster of stars: the planet Venus. Rapidly, it grew in size; became a disk and then a white globe.

Thora stared at the approaching planet with burning eyes. There she would find the goal of her desires – the gigantic interstellar radio station, constructed ten thousand years ago by the vanished Arkonide settlers who had erected a base on Venus with its automatic installations still functioning perfectly to this very day. And the frightening defense weapons of an unimaginable technology were still effectively protecting the Venusian radio station and the positronic brain.

Thora was well acquainted with the rules that governed the policy decisions and reactions of the positronic brain. Since destroyer C had been constructed according to Arkonide plans, it would fulfill all necessary prerequisites to be recognized as an Arkonide vessel when it would be probed and checked out by the barrier beams of the ancient fortress. No obstacles would be placed in its way when destroyer C would come in for a landing. Thora knew only too well the powerful fortifications and weaponry of this age-old Venusian base and what means the mighty positronic brain had at its disposal to defend itself.

After these deliberations her doubts were quickly dispelled and she said to R-17: 'We ought to start slowing down now.'

'We have already done so,' replied the robot. 'One can't notice it. The force fields are compensating for any change that has occurred in our speed. Look – Venus is growing larger!'

Indeed, the bright sphere had come very close and it seemed to increase in size steadily though only very gradually. A dense cloud cover made it impossible to catch even a glimpse of the planet's surface. But Thora did not need actually to see it, she knew that it resembled a primeval world. Immense oceans extended over a large part of the planet's face, which was mainly a maze of water, swamps and gigantic jungles. The extensive jungles were inhabited by giant saurian reptiles who had only comparatively recently conquered the continents.

The jungle was practically impassable for man. Even using the most sophisticated means of modern technology, to cover any distance on foot would be almost impossible. Whoever happened to be stranded in this jungle was doomed. Saurian giant lizards, swamps and carnivorous plants would soon finish them off.

The Venusian atmosphere was breathable for human beings. Despite its high carbon dioxide content it had sufficient oxygen for man. The upper strata of the atmosphere contained increasingly larger percentages of volcanic pollution and admixtures of inert, rare gases. The average daily temperature was close to 120° Fahrenheit. The constant dense cloud layer created a hothouse effect over the entire planet and gave rise to a vegetation growing in great profusion.

One full Venusian day lasted as long as 10 days on Earth. This meant 120 hours of uninterrupted daylight, which was followed by an equally long stretch of darkness. One Venusian year lasted 224.7 Earth-days.

Gravity and escape velocity were slightly less than on Earth but due to the planet's closer proximity to the sun it received a far greater share of the sun's warming rays.

Not a very pleasant world for man to live on but this is what Terra must have looked like millions of years ago. Some day this planet would be inhabited, maybe by some future generations of mankind who might change this fertile soil into a paradise.

For the time being, however, Venus was far removed from this utopian state. Planet of Hell was the name that Bell had called it once during a conversation with Thora. She was reminded of this name as the destroyer penetrated the upper strata of the atmosphere and kept slowly descending toward the planet's surface.

Their speed was greatly reduced now. Bright wisps of clouds passed by the window and appeared to drift upwards.

The radar screen indicated the presence of high mountain ranges. A plateau of such a mountain range was the location of the star station of the ancient Arkonides which housed the positronic brain and the hyperwave-sender.

Robot R-17 resumed control over the ship. He determined the position of their eventual destination. He had not been programmed by any command that forbade him to land the ship on the Venusian base. Suddenly they emerged from the bottom layer of the cloud bank. The destroyer seemed to have reached the lowest depths of a gaseous ocean and it was now flying almost directly above the bottom. The sun shone weakly like a dull spot through the gas masses but sufficiently strong to cause in them violent turbulences even though they rarely thrust down to the surface of the planet.

Thora looked down and shuddered. They had been flying across an ocean and were now approaching the coast. There was remarkably good visibility and far off toward the horizon towered high mountains with flattened tops. Dense vegetation seemed to cover the sides of these mountains halfway up. A whitish glow came from inside dark canyons. Thora knew that these were gigantic waterfalls rushing to the bottom of the abyss, providing new water supplies for the swamps in the jungle.

The jungle . . .

The continents seemed to be completely overgrown with these jungles. All she could see were the oceans, mountain ranges and the endless expanses of the jungle. One immense green carpet stretched wherever her eyes could see, only occasionally broken by some tall rocks and watery surfaces which glistened green and foreboding. Now and then this poisonous-looking surface would part to let appear a gigantic head which undulated aimlessly at the end of a long, sinuous neck, soon to dip down again below the surface.

The ship kept descending.

'Our destination is 500 miles from here,' R-17 stated without any emotion. 'Shall we land or turn back?'

'We'll land, of course,' replied Thora. Her voice sounded as calm as the robot's, although a storm of emotion was raging inside her. It was very difficult for her to keep herself under control. In a few hours she would know whether she had been able to outsmart Rhodan or not. 'Any sign yet of the sensor rays coming from the Venus Base?'

R-17 checked his instruments. 'No.'

We must still be too far away from it, thought Thora. She remembered that the barrier zone had a radius of

300 miles. The positronic brain inside the mountain fortress prohibited any unauthorized landings inside the barred area and would open fire on any trespassers without warning. Thora knew that she would not run such a risk because of her brainwave pattern that identified her as a member of the Arkonide ruling race. But of paramount importance was the fact that the ship was built according to typical Arkonide designs. Its built-in code transmitter would make certain that all inquiries from the positronic brain would be answered in the required manner.

'360 miles to go,' announced the robot mechanically.

Thora threw a glance at the weapon rack built into one of the walls of the cabin. In it were all kinds of hand weapons that might be needed in case of an emergency landing in unknown territory. She shrugged her shoulders. No need for those, she thought; what for?

'We are approaching the barrier zone,' said R-17.

Thora sat up straight in her chair and peered fascinated through the window down at the steaming surface of the Venusian hell. Nothing seemed to have changed since the time she had been here last. A fairly large lake glided by below them. Steep rockwalls ringed its shores. The rockwalls were overgrown with sparse vegetation.

Beyond she could see one of the many islands formed of high rocks, gigantic plateaus which reared up from the swampy morass. Life was relatively bearable up there.

'Descend farther!' ordered Thora, but she would have been hard put to explain the reasons for this command.

The robot obeyed silently. Their ship's altitude made no difference as far as the sensor rays of the station were concerned. They made contact with the ship, requested the identifying code signal – and received no reply. All this took place completely automatically and unnoticed by the two occupants of the ship, whose instruments only indicated that it had been tracked by the station's radar installation.

The rest came therefore as a total surprise.

Down below at the edge of the plateau a rocky ledge moved aside. From a dark cleft in the rock a shiny cannon barrel emerged; it was ringed by glittering spirals. The barrel raised up and pointed its orifice threateningly at the low-flying spaceship. Three hundred miles from this spot, impulse currents raced through complicated machinery, opened and closed contacts, activated relays and finally resulted in a positronic command. This was transmitted by a radio signal and reached the disintegrator cannon in the barrier zone.

Neither Thora nor R-17 had been prepared for a direct hit that had been fired at them without warning. The destructive energy ray dissolved the crystalline structural field of the ship and vaporized its matter.

R-17 automatically depressed the exit button.

The spacecraft's nose had been sliced away neatly from the ship's command center. The energy supply was still miraculously functioning. But the mechanism jammed.

Thora clung desperately to the back and sides of her armchair. The ship nosed down at an angle, tumbling crazily toward the green hell below. The cabin window was now below Thora. She realized that they would still land on the plateau – if this sudden crash could be called a landing.

If they were lucky, the tree tops might soften the impact on the ground.

Why did the positronic brain order us shot down? Thora asked herself in her last few lucid moments. Why?

Then she felt a violent blow that rammed her legs almost into her abdomen. The pain coursed through her entire body, up to her brain before she finally lost consciousness.

Robot R-17 hit his forehead against the instrument panel.

'WHAT A PROSPECT!'

Reginald Bell was sitting in the command center of the Ministry of Defense of the New Power. He had everything under control. All around him little lamps were glowing on instrument panels, videoscreens were flickering, visiphones were humming constantly as an uninterrupted stream of new reports kept arriving. All these reports concerned Thora's unexpected flight.

Next to Bell stood John Marshall, the telepath of the mutant corps. He had been born in Australia and had discovered fairly late in life his remarkable gift of being able to read other people's minds. It seemed inevitable that he had joined Perry Rhodan's forces and had become one of his most valuable collaborators. His talent for extrasensory perception had been caused by the effect of the increasing radioactivity of Earth's atmosphere on his parents' genes. There were many mutants like John Marshall but only a few among them knew about their talent. Even mutants needed a long time to become aware of their altered senses.

'He'll be here soon,' said John Marshall to Reginald Bell.

Khrest the Arkonide was standing in the back of the room. His tall figure loomed above the videoscreens and his whitish hair contrasted sharply with the dark control panels along the wall. His albino eyes had a reddish glint in them.

He was deeply embarrassed by Thora's flight. Deep inside, of course, he could understand her motives; nevertheless he regarded her reckless actions as unforgivable.

She had endangered Project Terra in a most irresponsible manner.

The race of the Arkonides had reached the zenith of their development and surpassed it. Their galactic empire that had taken thousands of years to establish was now decaying because of the Arkonide rulers' inactivity. Decadent and arrogant by nature, the Arkonides would some day become the victims of their own might.

Khrest had clearly forseen this course of events. He realized that these determined, fearless, vital earthlings would become the future heirs of the Arkonide empire – and he was convinced that it would fare well in their hands. Far better, in any case, than in the hands of those people who belonged to the colonial realm of the Arkonides but who had very little left in common with the human race despite their intelligence. Far better, too, than in the fins of the fish-like races inhabiting the Pleiades or the wings of the bird-lizards of the Rigel system. Let alone, naturally, the six-fingered claws of the Topides.

Khrest had searched for successors capable of taking over from his own decadent race and believed he had found them in the inhabitants of Terra. Perry Rhodan and Reginald Bell had received from him a special hypno-training which had supplied them with the superior knowledge and technology of his own Arkonide race. He had set about systematically to prepare Rhodan for his future task. Khrest liked secretly to refer to this plan as 'Project Terra.'

And now Thora had endangered this plan.

The door opened and Perry Rhodan entered the center. He greeted Khrest and Marshall with a slight nod, then turned to his friend Bell. 'Any news?'

'A lot of news, Perry. I don't know where to begin.'

'At the beginning, of course. Make it brief, will you, we don't have much time to waste.'

31

'Thora took off one hour ago with destroyer C, flew by the Moon in the direction of Venus. She responded everywhere with the correct identification signal. She must have the robot pilot on board with her. She was not stopped. If she has continued increasing her ship's velocity at the expected rate, she should have landed on Venus by now.'

'I can understand,' said Rhodan, 'how she felt, Reg. We have waited too long in keeping our promise to her. She must have been desperately longing to see Arkon again.'

'You are too generous in your thoughts,' interjected Khrest. 'I appreciate that you are speaking up for Thora here. But we must face things the way they really are. Whatever her motives might have been, the fact is that she acted wrong. If she should manage to get inside the station she will take over the hyperwave sender. She can do that as the former commander of our exploratory expedition. Just imagine the results!'

Rhodan remembered the defeated invasion of the vicious Mind Snatchers and he shuddered. If Thora should succeed in her plan to send a message to Arkon via hyperwave it would be spread instantaneously throughout the entire universe and most likely be intercepted by any number of alien belligerent races. This would indeed represent a grave danger. These hostile races could calculate the direction and distance from where the message originated. They would be very curious to determine where in that distant part of the galaxy a so far unknown inhabited system actually existed. They would come to Earth and find it unprepared, still divided and therefore ripe to be colonized by them.

What a frightening prospect!

'I wonder how she tricked the robot guards?' said Rhodan. 'Any information how she did it?'

'Yes,' blustered Bell. 'The guards report that she approached them in the usual official procedure, spoke with the pilot of destroyer C and then took off with him. They had not received any orders to stop Thora.'

'Of course not!' growled Rhodan. 'Who would ever have thought that Thora would break her word?'

This time it was Khrest who defended her. 'She must have believed she would never see Arkon again unless she resorted to such a ruse.'

'I am inclined to believe,' said Rhodan with a hint of a smile, 'that there were some additional motives in her case. Just think of the planet of eternal life. The Immortal made it possible for me to obtain periodically a prolongation of my life and also gave me permission to pass this on to any Earthman whom I would consider worthy of such a fabulous gift. The Arkonides were not included in this offer because their race had already reached the zenith of its existence and was on a downward grade. The human race, on the other hand, was on an ascending path in its development. Thora is proud and arrogant. She could not bear to be humbled like that and therefore wanted to avenge herself in her own peculiar way. She wanted to prove to me that she is the stronger of us two. She does not seem to have any idea – or maybe she does not care – about the horrible consequences for mankind. Her desire to return home is understandable but not her obvious stupidity or lack of consideration.'

'What are you going to do about it, Rhodan?'

Bell sat up and listened attentively. He was eagerly awaiting Rhodan's reply, at least as much as Khrest. Rhodan spoke slowly: 'I shall take up pursuit with destroyer A and will go after Thora right away. John Marshall and Son Okura will come with me. Get us a car, Reg, will you! Anything else we need we'll find on board the destroyer.'

Khrest made a weak effort to protest but quickly resigned himself again into inactivity. It was still hard for him to get used to the Earthmen's speedy reactions – all this vitality still overwhelmed him.

Bell's reaction was quite different. He cocked his head and said: 'And how about me?' with an expression that would have suited a little boy who had not been remembered with presents at Christmastime. 'Am I supposed to stay here and just twiddle my thumbs?'

'Not a bad idea.' Rhodan jokingly accepted this suggestion. 'Relax, Reggie, you'll follow me with destroyer B as soon as possible. Unfortunately we cannot cancel the announced festivities without a good excuse. That means you'll have to stand in for me. If I'm not mistaken, Col Freyt has already announced your address on TV. I hope you'll be up to it and have some prepared speech somewhere up your sleeve.'

'I'm supposed to give a speech?' said Bell highly indignant, and his ruddy cheeks blushed even deeper. 'What about?'

'What else but about the manner in which Earth could be defended in case of an interstellar invasion by hostile aliens. A very timely topic, don't you think? The moment the festivities are over you'll start out after me. Is that a deal, Reg?'

'A deal.' Bell did not sound too enthusiastic. He was afraid he might miss some of the fun in that interplanetary chase.

'Inform Son Okura!' requested Rhodan.

Bell was still not too happy. 'Why Okura of all people?' he asked while he was already busy getting in touch with the command center of the mutant corps.

'He's our frequency seer, as you know. Because his eyes can perceive all visible as well as invisible waves and especially the infra-red rays. This makes him invaluable during night time. Remember that night lasts on Venus as long as five Earth days. Besides, he can "see" heat radia-

34

tion; even hours after some warm body has left the area, he can still "see" it as clear as a picture. You agree, don't you, that we couldn't find a better man for this job than Son Okura?'

Bell had meanwhile made his requests of the mutant corps command center via radio. Now he had calmed down as he suggested: 'You are right, Perry. But he can't run very fast. How about taking along a teleporter?'

'*You* can bring one along later. There's room for only three men in a destroyer. I'll even have to leave our robot pilot behind.'

'Why don't you take a larger ship?'

Rhodan thought for a little while. 'That's a splendid idea. You'll follow me not with our third destroyer but take an auxiliary vessel of the class of the *Good Hope*. Be sure to bring along enough mutants. But I almost believe all these precautions will not be necessary.' Rhodan smiled mischievously. 'All will be over anyhow by the time you get there.'

Bell gasped for air but then quickly changed his mind. He cast a glance in Khrest's direction, remembering that the serious Arkonide scientist never had shown great appreciation for his own peculiar brand of humor. He suppressed whatever wisecrack had been on the tip of his tongue and simply said: 'Yes, let's hope so.'

While Bell was still standing in front of the TV cameras addressing a world-wide audience, destroyer A was racing out into space. The automatic pilot system would rapidly bring up the ship's velocity to almost the speed of light and then just as swiftly slow down again. Their course had been set.

Rhodan was sitting in the pilot's seat. To his right was Marshall and to his left the Japanese. Son Okura was wearing narrow-rimmed glasses. What irony of fate that he

35

of all men, who was the only one able to perceive invisible
light waves, had to depend on spectacles if he wanted to
recognize any objects in ordinary daylight. He had very
poor eyesight under normal circumstances. He had used
to work as an optician in a camera factory before Bell's
search troops had discovered him and he had subsequently
joined Rhodan's mutant corps. Now, finally, his hour had
come to help the New Power with his special talent.

'Do you think Thora will land close to the station?'
asked Marshall.

'Sounds logical to me,' replied Rhodan seriously. 'She
plans to inform Arkon of our planet's existence so that
they will come and rescue her from her exile. The hyperwave sender is inside the station. It stands to reason that
this is where she will land.'

'I have been on Venus some time ago,' remarked Son
Okura in his formal and rather reserved manner. 'This is
where I received my training as a mutant. It's not a very
pleasant place to be, if I may say so.'

'We have no choice in the matter, Okura,' said Rhodan.
'But on the other hand, I don't think there will be much
of a chance that we will ever get near those jungles. As
soon as we touch down at the base, I'll give my counter
orders to the positronic brain. Let's hope that Thora has
not yet gotten as far as the transmitter, so she can be
stopped in time.'

'Let's hope we won't be too late,' murmured Marshall
and gritted his teeth. 'I'd rather not think what might
happen otherwise.'

Rhodan looked straight ahead, where Venus had grown
from a bright point of light to a bright disk.

'Yes,' he agreed in a matter of fact voice, 'it would be
a catastrophe.'

Then all were silent for a while.

It did not take long before Venus increased even more

in size and they finally descended into the planet's atmosphere. The direction finders located the station and by then they found that night was about to fall. Soon it would be totally dark – five long Earth days.

For the moment this did not present any worry but Rhodan was very pleased in any case to have taken along Okura on this mission.

He checked the instrument panel.

'The station is 900 miles to the west from here. We'll descend closer to the surface to get better visibility. If I only knew how far Thora has gotten by now.'

Nobody answered.

Below the ship they could see the roof of the jungle which seemed to speed toward the now darkening eastern sky. They flew across a small primeval ocean, then a higher mountain range and finally again jungles and swamps.

'500 miles to go!'

Far ahead of them the horizon became hazy and seemed to meld into the cloud cover. Beyond they saw a dark red spot hovering in the milky mass – the setting sun. It would be five days before it would rise again in the east.

'Another 350 miles,' said Rhodan. 'We'll be at the barrier zone within five minutes.'

Marshall said calmly: 'We've made it safely to the base.'

But he was wrong.

He was just as wrong as Thora had been some time earlier.

Once again the electronic guard installation inside the ancient Arkonide base came to life. Once again the sensors spotted the new arrival and probed it with their far reaching sensitive fingers. Once again the request to respond to the identification signal remained unanswered. The request was repeated but destroyer A did not reply.

Rhodan had forgotten that the special code installations of the three destroyers had not yet been positronically prepared. An understandable oversight in the hastily undertaken pursuit but with catastrophic results, even if at the same time it prevented Thora from reaching her destination.

The ship was unable to carry out any defensive measures for Rhodan was blinded by the sudden flash of the disintegrator ray. He could feel a powerful concussion race through the ship's metal body. He was jolted upwards, jerked out of his seat. The horizon seemed to reel crazily as the destroyer crashed toward the ground.

Fortunately, only the ship's rear had been hit by the disintegrator beam. The engines had been destroyed but the front and command center had remained undamaged.

Rhodan's fist automatically flew down hard onto the exit button.

Unlike earlier in destroyer C, here the whole mechanism was still working. The entire command center was ejected from the destroyer and stabilized itself horizontally thanks to its anti-grav projectors. The emergency jets began to work at once and propelled the central cabin sideways and out of the barrier zone. This saved them from further bombardment from the station's disintegrator cannons.

The roof of the jungle came slowly nearer. Treacherous looking swamp pools seemed to emit a weak irridescent light. The sudden silence was rent by the dull roar of a saurian whose voice penetrated the cracked cabin wall. Something moved clumsily down below in the morass. Okura, who sat quite still, his eyes fixed on the uncertain depth below, began to shudder.

'Oh, those beasts!' he groaned. 'They have got wind of their prey.'

'That's just a figure of speech, I hope,' said Marshall.

The Japanese did not reply. He knew the Venusian jungle only too well.

The emergency aggregate of the command center, which

38

now had been separated from the ship itself, made the small Arkonide reactors work ceaselessly to produce corpuscle streams sufficient to brake the ship's downward fall. The cabin floated toward the ground much slower than if it had been carried by an emergency parachute.

Off to one side, Rhodan saw the rest of the destroyer tumble toward the ground. It had remained still inside the barrier zone. Another direct hit split it neatly in half. All matter near the point of impact was instantly vaporized so that two big fragments finally tore a hole in the jungle roof. Strong branches broke the fall of the two pieces that eventually came to rest a few feet above the filthy matted jungle floor.

'Hope we won't land in some lake,' said Okura. He sounded very worried; he must be terribly afraid of the saurians.

'This cabin will float,' Rhodan tried to comfort his frightened companion. Rhodan glanced around the cabin. 'If only our weapons have all been placed in their proper places in our weapon rack! The destroyer was not yet fully equipped, not quite ready for take-off. Our crash is ample proof of that. The code installation was incomplete. Let's hope we'll have better luck with our arms. . .'

'We don't have a radio transmitter.'

'Just the tiny transmitters in the all-purpose bracelets. But they are too weak, their signals can't reach Earth.'

They were now at an altitude of about 300 feet and could already make out their probable landing area. There were no special irregular features in the landscape, no swamp lakes, no rock outcroppings, only the undulating roof of the virgin forest.

'I don't expect any problems – at least not during the landing,' stated Rhodan in a firm voice. 'I wish I could say the same for later on. . .'

The highest treetops came closer. Rhodan was fully

aware that the actual ground was still much farther below. The tree trunks of the jungle giants often had a diameter of 40-50 feet and could reach a height up to 450 feet. In between 'and on them grew a profusion of parasitic plants also considerably bigger than their counterparts in the jungles of the Earth.

The cabin floor touched the first branches and slowly dipped down into the relatively soft nest formed by the leaves of the treetops. The reactors were still working and still braking the cabin's fall.

And then the cabin came to a halt.

It rested at a tilted angle in the midst of the green ocean. Dusk began to fall and colored the eternal cloud banks in dark, almost black shades. From the west came the glow of the sunset as if the sky had caught on fire, threatening to burn up the entire planet.

Rhodan waited no longer; he switched off the aggregates. All at once the cabin's normal weight returned, putting a heavy load on the supporting branches. Some of these could not withstand the sudden change in pressure and broke off, while others bent steeply downwards. The cabin began to slide down.

Before Rhodan could manage to correct the situation, the entire cabin crashed toward the jungle floor, twisting and tumbling until some horrifying seconds later it came to rest again among some branches about two feet thick.

Now they had finally landed on Venus.

A few minutes passed. John Marshall awoke from his superficial unconsciousness. His forehead hurt and his first thought was that it would be a long time until their search for Thora would be completed. He sat up and noticed Okura bending over Rhodan and carefully examining his head. He intercepted the thoughts of the Japanese and knew at once what had happened.

Okura turned around. 'He is badly cut. He hit his face

against something. Very hard. All is bloody. Hope it won't be serious . . .'

Marshall quickly regained his strength. He got to his feet, held onto the cabin wall and walked toward Okura. Rhodan lay stretched out on the cabin floor, breathing weakly.

The Japanese staggered to his feet. The cabin floor was at a slant; one had to get used to it. He found bandages and medicines in the medicine cabinet on the wall. Rhodan received an injection of some powerful stimulant, antibiotics and fever depressants. Soon his shallow breathing became regular again. The two men placed him on two seats that had been pushed together to form a provisional bed where a beneficial sleep would work its cure.

Okura dressed Marshall's wounds before he began to worry about himself. 'Of course, it'd get my legs again,' he said with resignation. 'It always will affect my legs. I have so much trouble already just plain walking. I'm afraid I'll be a burden to you when we have to march through the jungle.'

Marshall grew pale. 'You don't seriously consider that we might have to go down there?' and he pointed to the ground. 'Down into that hell full of giant spiders and reptiles – and God knows what all other creatures crawling around there. No! Ten horses won't drag me off this tree. Here at least we are relatively safe.'

'True enough,' smiled the Japanese politely. 'You won't starve here. But you are also safe in prison.'

John Marshall did not know what to answer.

He turned his glance away from Rhodan and looked through the window down into the uncertain green twilight.

He thought he saw, far down below, a giant shadow amble by. From somewhere came a bellowing roar.

Despite the heat, Marshall felt suddenly chilled.

* * *

Several hours later, when Perry Rhodan looked at himself in a mirror, he was frightened.

There was a huge abrasion straight across his brow; it would take weeks until this wound would heal without the special Arkonide organ-plasma. His right eye was all swollen; he had trouble recognizing his own face.

He sighed in disgust and leaned back in his chair so that the Japanese could put a new bandage over his injuries. 'My best friends won't be able to recognize me,' he said 'That'll at least give Bell something to kid me about.'

'He'd better not do that as long as I am around,' threatened Marshall, 'or I'll break his bones.'

'That's easier said than done,' warned Rhodan. 'There's a lot of fat wrapped around those bones; they are well cushioned.' He waited until Okura had finished his job, then added: 'What's our situation now?'

Okura stepped back and appraised his handiwork as a good Samaritan. 'Your injuries are not dangerous. But the sad fact is that we are stuck in the middle of the Venusian jungle without any means of getting in touch with Earth. We have lost our spaceship and with it all possibility of making contact with the Radiant Dome inside our base on this planet. So we will have to depend entirely on our own resources. We must somehow reach the station – or else we'll have to wait it out till Bell finds us by sheer accident.'

'We have our mini-transmitters,' interjected Marshall.

'They won't be of much help; their range is very limited. When we ejected with the center from the rest of the ship we were cut off from our means of communication, our radio transmitters. That should teach us a lesson for the future. From now on we must make sure that each ejector emergency capsule is equipped with its own radio installation. As far as Bell is concerned we can of course establish communication with him provided his ship accidentally comes within our range. Should we wait for this eventu-

42

ality while Thora mobilizes all the horrors of the universe?'

'Okura is right with his analysis of our situation, Marshall,' commented Rhodan. 'There is only one choice open to us: we must try to forestall whatever Thora is planning to do. We must prevent her from getting inside the base. But I have no reason to believe that she has fared any better than we did in her attempt to get inside the barrier zone. She flew here with the same type destroyer that was at the identical stage of construction as ours. The code installations of her ship had not yet been properly programmed – just like ours. Let's hope that she survived the crashlanding of her spacecraft.'

Marshall snarled furiously. 'I wouldn't mind if she broke her neck.'

'I wouldn't wish that on any one,' answered Rhodan in a reproachful tone. 'Never wish bad luck on another person, just prevent them from causing ill harm to others. And besides, it wouldn't do us much good even if Thora should break her neck: we'd still be marooned here in the jungle on Venus.'

'I didn't really mean it that way,' apologized Marshall. 'All I wanted to say was that I see red when I think of what that alien vixen has done to us – even if she is beautiful.'

'I'm glad you can still be objective on *that* point,' Okura grinned mischievously.

Rhodan raised himself while holding onto the wall for support. He was still dizzy from his long period of unconsciousness. While his companions kept a watchful eye on him he slowly groped along the wall till he reached the window. He looked out into the bleak darkness of the Venusian night. But even if it had been bright daylight, Rhodan would not have dared leave his cabin. Apart from the dangers lurking in the hardly ever explored wilderness, he was far too weak to risk the hardships of marching through the primeval forest.

And yet – each additional hour of delay would increase the imminent collapse of all he had accomplished up to this moment. True, Col Freyt could substitute for him; but once the news would spread that Rhodan, President of the New Power, had not returned from a flight to Venus, and that in all likelihood he had made a fine dinner morsel for one of the Venusian giant lizards – no, Rhodan could not even bear to think of the potential grave consequence. The hardly abated fierce chauvinism of some ambitious politicians was bound to 'save their fatherland' and with it the Terranians would revert to simple Earthlings. And that was the worst fate that could befall them. They would recede once again to the level of narrow-minded nationalism and thus be helplessly at the mercy of an alien invasion.

This realization permitted only one decision. Rhodan expressed it to his two companions: 'We have to reach the base. We'll have another rest period. A good sleep will restore our strength – then we'll march off. We have no special Arkonide protectitve suits and not enough food. How about arms?'

Okura opened the door of a built-in weapon cabinet. There were three pulse-ray guns neatly stored in a rack. Otherwise the cabinet was empty.

'That's at least something,' growled Marshall. 'They work fine on saurian reptiles, I was told.'

This was apparently though not Rhodan's greatest concern – how to shoot Venusian saurians. 'No machineguns? No rifles?' He looked around. 'How much food and water do we have?'

'A few sticks of food concentrates and a couple of gallons of water. Enough for several days. We could hunt for food, shoot some lizards.'

'Wrong!' Rhodan shook his head. 'The energy beam of a positronic pulse-ray burns and vaporizes instantly any matter. There wouldn't be much left to eat even if we should get one of those giant monsters.'

'Then we must make sure we only kill the beast,' said Marshall, 'and stop the energy beam in time. Besides, you know that I always carry my trusty old revolver. Bell has made fun of me more than once because of that, I'm sure you remember.'

'I certainly do and I share his opinion,' laughed Rhodan. 'How do you propose to use that toy against a saurian?'

'It doesn't have to be one of those giant monsters,' countered Marshall. 'There are plenty of smaller animals in the jungle. Probably much tastier, too.'

That seemed to make sense to Okura. 'Marshall has a point there, sir. I'm sure we can hunt for meat and there must also be some fruit growing here. I can remember frequently eating some strange local fruit at the time of my training here. I am quite confident I can recognize it if I see it again. I am much more worried about our water supply. We can't possibly drink that gunk from the swamps. Who knows what fine bacteria we would pick up there.'

'Oh, that's nothing,' Rhodan reassured him. 'We don't need to boil the water, there is some germicide in this cabinet. We pour the powder into the water and it will kill all the bacteria in it. We still will have to filter the water to get rid of any poisonous properties. And if we should run out of the powder then we still can boil the water. There is plenty of wood around here.'

'Yes, and plenty wet and damp. We won't have much luck with it.'

'What are you talking about wood for all the time?' said Okura. 'Who needs it? Look here!' With these words he reached for a small package in the storage cabinet and held it up. 'See, Marshall! Energite! One hundred times more efficient than dry heat cubes. We have enough here for three meals a day for the next three months. All we need now are the lizard cutlets.'

Marshall made a face. 'Brrr . . . lizard meat! Some delicacy!'

'How do you know if you never tasted it? It's about time you find out for yourself!' Rhodan admonished the skeptical telepath. Then he sat down again on his provisional couch. 'Pack everything that we might need. Then lie down and sleep. Who knows when we'll get another chance to sleep in relative safety and comfort.'

Rhodan closed his eyes and soon his deep regular breathing revealed that he was determined to gather up all his strength for the coming adventure.

An adventure that from one second to the next would hurl them from an era of the most modern technology back into the most primitive conditions.

They were suspended in the thick foliage and branches of a giant tree more than 150 feet above the treacherous floor of the jungle. Creeper plants, as thick as an arm, facilitated their downward climb.

Rhodan cast one last glance back into the cabin whose shelter and security they were now leaving for good. He estimated that the Arkonide base with its robot crew must lie some 310 miles due west from them. An almost insurmountable distance because of the primordial fauna and flora.

He checked the pulse-ray gun in his belt, hung a small bag with his share of water and food concentrates around his neck, and groped for the next branch. Marshall had already descended several yards down the tree.

Okura stared down into the dark with utmost concentration. 'We are lucky. A small clearing No trace of animals.'

As usual, even Rhodan felt uncanny when he observed how well the mutant could see in almost total darkness. He himself could hardly recognize his own hand right in front of his eyes.

Somewhere in the distance a volcano seemed to have erupted; perhaps in the next mountain range. A weak, reddish glow spread throughout the jungle, bathing everything in a pink diffuse light. But this could be hardly called 'seeing.'

Rhodan fumbled with his foot for a halt, found it, then let himself slowly down along a creeper plant. He almost believed it would be easier and faster for them to travel along the treetops than down below on the treacherous jungle floor. But they would only know for sure after they had tried both methods. Maybe they could change their mode of travel during the daylight hours.

It took three hours till their feet touched solid ground.

Okura looked at the compass on his all-purpose wristband. 'Let's go that way,' he declared. 'That's the direction of the base. Let's hope we won't find any obstacles in our way. As far as I can see there are not any swamps around here. And the ground is relatively dry.'

Rhodan's head hurt. Even an immortal gets headaches, he thought bitterly. And he can even die, if he is unlucky.

While he was marching behind Okura, all the events on the Planet of Eternal Life passed in quick review in his mind's eye like a film. They had pursued the trail that led through the galaxy and time to Wanderer, the lonely planet on which the immortal being from the past resided. 'It' had explained to Rhodan, at least partially, the secret of everlasting cell preservation. *It* had also granted him an opportunity to submit himself to the so-called 'cell-shower.' This caused the process of aging to be arrested for a certain period of time – exactly 62 terrestrial years. *It* had decreed that only Earthlings were permitted to use this cell shower, and only those that were given permission by Perry Rhodan.

Reginald Bell was the only other person to have benefitted from this life-prolonging process.

In another 62 years Perry Rhodan would calculate the exact space coördinates of the wandering planet with the help of the great positronic brain. Then he would return to the planet Wanderer and receive another cell shower. But six decades is a long time. Many things might happen during this period . . .

Okura stopped suddenly. He peered intensely into the dark, then reached back his arm to feel Rhodan. Marshall had run into Rhodan and cursed under his breath, 'What's the matter?'

Okura whispered, 'There's something moving up there in front of us, a large shadow. I can't recognize what it is. It makes no noise.'

'Then it can't be a saurian lizard. You can hear those for miles.'

Rhodan was silent. He listened attentively. His hand moved instinctively to the gun in his belt.

The Japanese breathed a sigh of relief. 'Probably some other animal. Anyhow, it can't see as well as I do, because it hasn't noticed us. Now it's making a right turn and moving away from us. It was about the size of a gorilla and looked very much like one, too. Maybe there are already apes on Venus.'

'Oh, for heaven's sake!' said Marshall softly.

Rhodan turned around. 'Why? Do you have something against apes?'

'No, but if apes really exist here, then our colonists on Venus will have a lot of trouble with the Venusians – in another 100,000 years, that is.'

Rhodan chuckled. 'I'd like to have your worries, Marshall. Is that all that's bothering you now?'

Marshall mumbled something incomprehensible, not giving a proper reply. Okura continued to advance. Rhodan once more held his hands in front of his face to protect it and followed the Japanese.

The night would continue for four more Earth days and if they did not run into any unexpected difficulties they could make about 60 miles before the next sunrise.

What a prospect!

Five hours later Rhodan stretched out his arm and seized Okura by the shoulder. 'We must pause here. We must be cautious with our strength, we must use it wisely otherwise we'll never reach our destination. As soon as we get to some suitable spot we'll camp and rest. Maybe we'll find a clearing in the jungle.'

'May I suggest something else?' The Japanese had stopped. 'We might climb a few yards up some tree. We are bound to find a big branch with enough room for all of us to sit on. Down here on the ground I would have to be continually on the lookout for dangerous animals. I think we will be relatively safe up in the trees.'

'I am surprised we didn't get into any swampy area yet,' Marshall mused. 'We lucked out so far.'

'But we made just barely three miles in all this time,' said Rhodan.

Okura spotted a suitable tree and began to climb up. Thirty feet off the ground he found a broad, horizontal branch, completely overgrown by a nest of creeper plants which formed a kind of cave. The men crawled inside and felt somewhat protected.

Marshall took over as cook. Soon the food concentrates had dissolved in the boiling water and they sniffed an appetizing odor of hot soup coming from the steaming kettle. It made them almost feel at home in the wilderness.

'Things aren't so bad after all,' said Marshall, much more cheerful now, stirring the soup. 'When day breaks we'll make good time and maybe even enjoy our hike through the jungle.'

He could not see Rhodan's worried face. He remained silent. After a while Okura broke the silence. 'But it isn't day yet.'

Marshall said nothing more. He just kept stirring his soup in silence.

DARK NIGHTMARE

Many hours earlier.

A hazy sun was about to set on the Venusian horizon. The pale disk beyond the misty cloud layers was diminishing in light intensity while at the same time it became more colorful. The weak rays of the sun were refracted in their course through the cloud veils and changed the whole western sky into a magnificent spectral color display.

Gradually red shades began to dominate everything. The primeval landscape was enveloped in a pink haze and the green hell of the treacherously glittering surface of the swamp seemed to become a riot of colors on the palette of a celestial artist who was watching from some invisible vantage point over his constantly changing work.

All life on Venus seemed to hold its breath for a bit with the onset of the long Venusian night which, so to speak, was ushered in by a changing of the guards. The mighty saurians came out of the woods to return to the security of their former watery home. Entire herds were pouring and trampling through the tall reeds along the shore, turning the bright iridescence of the swamp into a whirling, gigantic spectrum resembling colorful galaxies that travel on their endless orbits in the void, forever spinning in their futile quest for a destination.

In the distance glowed the bare rocks of the mountain ranges. They looked as if liquid fire had been poured upon them. In between glittered silvery bright waterfalls. Wherever they hit the canopy of the jungle, way down below, their waters would scatter in fine sprays forming one immense rainbow sheath that covered the world with a transparent colorful veil.

While the saurians went to their long night of rest, the nocturnal inhabitants of the jungle world began to awaken. The brief pause during the transition was abruptly terminated as the sun sank below the misty and burning horizon. Accompanied by a cacaphony of shrill cawing, giant birds flew on silent wings through the twilight, hunting for food. Gigantic moths fluttered toward the sinking sun, trying in vain to catch up with it.

At the edge of the rocky plateau, which reared up like an island from the green jungle ocean, stood several men watching the mighty spectacle of nature with deep emotion. Although the sight was nothing new for them, they could never quite escape its magic spell.

They were all dressed in a similar fashion – or rather, they used to wear the same kind of clothes. Their uniforms by now were torn; their belts were the only thing that kept their rags from falling off their bodies. Their tattered trouser legs were tucked in their worn-out boots. Some of the men had wrapped animal skins around their shoulders to protect them against the cold that always accompanied the onset of night.

Their hair was long, their beards matted. But even despite their peculiar appearance there was no mistaking them for anything but inhabitants of the planet Earth.

One of them, a powerfully built, short man with a broad face, shielded his eyes with his right hand. 'It's much more beautiful here than on Earth,' he said in a language that sounded like Russian. 'Perhaps this has induced the others to want to stay here.'

'Most likely, General Tomisenkow. There is no other explanation. They have lost their minds.'

The former commander of the Eastern air landing division, recently defeated by Rhodan's forces, energetically shook his head.

'I don't believe their actions could be so simply explained. There might be other, more complicated reasons for their decision. Venus is a savage world where freedom reigns ...'

'Aren't we also free men here?' asked one of the men.

'Freedom and freedom – there can be a world of difference between them. Isn't freedom a relative concept depending greatly on the political dogma of whoever talks about it? You can order men to be free but they can also fight to obtain it.'

'These are strange words, general,' said another man and gazed across to a wide plain extending over to the west. There, too, similar little island plateaus jutted out from the jungle. A column of smoke rose from one of the mesas. 'Didn't the rebels use the identical words?'

'Yes, they did. And they did even more than that: they separated from us because they no longer wished to return to Earth after our invasion here had failed. We were under orders to conquer Rhodan's Venusian base. We were unable to take his fortress. Rhodan then destroyed our ships and left us stranded and helpless in this wilderness. He knew that survival would be possible here for us. The rebels know that too. They have based their decision on this fact. We are not traitors, we want to get back to Earth in order to prepare for another invasion. But the rebels made up their minds to remain here and colonize Venus. They don't seem to realize how futile their efforts are since they start out with such a handicap, with practically nothing.'

'They managed to clear their island and to plant some fields. Venusian soil is very fertile. It would be a new frontier for settlers from Earth.'

'That might well be,' admitted the general unwillingly. 'But the fact still remains: they are mutineers breaking the law. And rebels should be hanged.'

The disheveled soldier next to Tomisenkow instinctively

touched his neck as if to reassure himself it was still connected to his head. His right hand rested firmly on the raygun butt in his belt. His eyes narrowed as he kept steadily looking over to the camp of the rebels. It was still light enough to be able to recognize all details there with field glasses. He could see the sentries on the rebel island as they were watching them in turn. The two groups were the only human beings on Venus. They belonged to the same power bloc on Earth – still they had become deadly enemies, fighting against each other.

General Tomisenkow was just about to turn away, to return to his hut, when suddenly a blinding flash of lightning rent the evening dusk. The bolt seemed to have struck the center of the plateau where the defeated, stranded invasion troops had found refuge. Thunderstorms were nothing unusual here on Venus but this was not the right time for them.

A front of compressed air swept over the men with a thundering rumble, throwing several men to the ground. Tomisenkow managed to cling to a tree. He stared into the night sky, trying to make out a glowing point which was sinking slowly earthwards like a giant meteor.

He couldn't believe his eyes – it looked like a spaceship!

But it could not be one of Rhodan's fleet; after all, this ship had been attacked and shot down by the hellish defense installations of the alien fortress that belonged to Rhodan.

Reinforcements from home? Of course. That must be the only possible explanation.

Before Tomisenkow could arrive at a decision there was another blinding flash. The crashing ship was not hit by it but it disappeared among the treetops of the jungle roof.

Another wave of compressed air followed. Then Tomisenkow ran back to his men. 'Sgt Rabow, take some men and try to find the crashed ship. In case you don't find any survivors, we can certainly use their provisions and weapons. Hurry, before it gets completely dark!'

The sergeant, a short, dark-haired man with quick eyes, nodded eagerly. 'I'll take our spotlight along, general. We'll track down that ship, rest assured. Don't you want to come along?'

Tomisenkow frowned. Disgusting how little discipline remained. It was high time to check these familiarities that were becoming more and more frequent among his soldiers. 'I have more important things to deal with right now,' he snarled furiously, as he walked off in the direction of the huts at the foot of a small rocky cone. He felt very lonely here among his men.

Sgt Rabow followed him with his eyes. They were thin slits now, making him look like a Mongolian. But he was no Oriental; he came from White Russia, a wiry Ukranian. And many of his compatriots had joined the rebel camp. Well, at the next opportunity . . .

He dismissed these thoughts and followed the general, keeping a respectful distance. The sentries remained at the edge of the plateau, waiting for the next flash from the fortress' defenses. But they were waiting in vain.

Thora awoke. It was completely dark. Her legs were still hurting and she could move them only with great effort. There was a shooting pain in her hips but it was bearable.

Cautiously, Thora tried to get up. She supported herself by holding onto the arms of her chair – finally she stood up. The floor beneath her feet was slanting at a steep angle; she had to watch out not to lose her balance.

She flipped the light but all remained dark. She slammed down hard on the lever of the emergency battery. The light came on immediately.

Her eyes fell on robot R-17. He was still leaning in the same posture in his seat, his forehead resting on the instrument panel. His right arm lay at a crazy angle on the narrow table in front of the console, while his left arm dangled toward the floor.

Thora felt very lonely all of a sudden, as she was considering the possibility that R-17 might be 'dead.' True, she could make small repairs, but in case one of the complicated inner positronic parts had been damaged, R-17 would remain forever in the Venusian jungle, rusting away during the course of centuries – unless he was found before then.

It was dark outside the cabin window. Only far off on the horizon a faint reddish glow stained the sky where long before the sun had set. The black silhouettes of rocks and trees stood out sharply against this pastel background.

Thora observed that she had not landed in the middle of the primeval forest. The destroyed ship had come to rest on flat ground. It was a miracle how the ship must have first broken its fall when it hit the jungle treetops, then slowly glided down until it reached the ground. The final impact, though, had still been hard enough to sprain her legs and condemn R-17 to immobility.

She stretched all her limbs. Nothing serious, nothing broken. Then she concentrated on the robot. With skilled hands she detached his breastplate and shone her flashlight into the maze of transistors, other electronic miniaturized parts and wiring. As far as she could determine, nothing was damaged. She replaced the breastplate, made sure that the magnetic locks had snapped shut tight. There was no doubt in her mind now, after this examination, where the trouble must have occurred: the robot had smashed his forehead against the instrument panel.

The headplate was just as easily removed and Thora saw at once how lucky she had been. One of the main wires had come loose and dangled uselessly among the tiny Arkonite tubes.

She found a soldering iron in the tool box and had the damage repaired within a few minutes. R-17 was at once wide awake. He raised his head, looked at Thora and asked: 'What happened? I must have become deactivated.'

'Just a wire, that was all. We were shot down by the guard cannons of the station. Probably something was wrong with the code remitter. The station should be about 900 miles from here. What next?'

'Wait,' answered R-17. That was the only sensible solution to the problem as far as he was concerned. He had lots of time.

'Wait? Wait for what? Until they find us? Venus is uninhabited. In case Rhodan has followed me he will fly directly to the station. It will not even occur to him that I might have been shot down. How is it with our transmitter?'

R-17 got to his feet and walked, leaning forward very strangely, to the door leading to the ship's radio station. His slanting posture was affected by the stabilizer gyroscope that was not functioning again. He adjusted to the slant of the ground and was independent of the center of gravity.

Thora stayed behind and tried to make out any details of the objects outside the cabin window. She noticed that it was growing darker, but only very gradually. The twilight period of Venus lasted five times longer than on Earth, therefore her eyes could adjust sufficiently to recognize more and more of her surroundings.

The ship rested at a slant on a small rock-strewn clearing. Occasional trees ringed the edge of the forest, which did not resemble the swampy lowlands of the jungle. That was a comforting thought.

R-17 returned to the command center. 'Our transmitter is out of order, it cannot be repaired,' he announced in his matter of fact voice devoid of any human emotions. 'This means we cannot count on any help unless we're missed very soon. Rhodan has been informed of our test flight, I assume.'

'No, Rhodan knows nothing about it – at least not until the moment we started. I left without authorization. I intend to establish communication with Arkon once I reach the Venusian base. Rhodan did not know that Khrest and I planned to return home to Arkon.'

The robot stopped in the middle of the room. He stared at the woman out of his crystalline lenses. 'You have acted against Rhodan's orders? You know that I have been conditioned to obey only Rhodan's commands. Therefore you have become my opponent.'

'We are both in the same situation.'

'Nevertheless, you must be punished.'

Thora's pride was hard hit. She, member of a ruling race, was being told by an object of her own creation that she deserved to be punished. The Terranian Rhodan had removed her own race's power over their robots.

'Yes, Rhodan ought to punish me,' she conceded, trying to sound still logical. 'But he can punish me only if he can lay his hands on me alive. It is your duty, consequently, to bring me back to Rhodan – to the Venus station. For this is where we shall find him.'

Robot R-17 could see that she was right in her argument. 'Well, then, let's proceed to the station and wait there for him.'

That, of course, was easier said than done.

'From now on I am responsible for your safety and for your life,' stated R-17 soberly. 'You have broken Rhodan's laws and have therefore become my prisoner. The destroyer is wrecked; we must start out immediately to avoid losing any unnecessary time.'

'How about food and water?' asked Thora.

The robot pointed to some built-in wall cabinets. 'There

are weapons, medications, water and food concentrates – all prepared for three persons. You will have enough therefore for almost two weeks. You are allowed to take along one hand weapon since this suits my purposes.'

Thora swallowed hard. A robot gave *her*, an Arkonide, permission to carry arms! She made up her mind right then and there to have R-17 put out of commission and broken down to his smallest components in the robot salvage yard at the earliest opportunity that would present itself.

She took the pulse-ray gun and put it in her belt. Then she packed the food concentrates into a small bag, handed it to the robot and took the first aid kit and medications. R-17 volunteered to carry the water container.

'I'll take along the searchlight,' decided Thora, and shuddered, picturing the dark nightmare of the Venusian jungle. Had she not been possessed by the notion of having to reach the station at all costs as quickly as possible, she would have waited for daybreak – five Earth days later. But she realized that each wasted minute lessened her chances to get in touch with Arkon. Rhodan was certain not to remain inactive on Earth and await the outcome of her flight to Venus.

'I can see very well in the dark,' R-17 reassured her. 'All I need to do is switch on my infra-red device. And if we should run into some hostile creatures I can use my neutron ray-gun.' He lifted his left arm to remind her of the built-in super weapon. 'I shall bring you safely to the fortress.'

The thought of the mighty saurians that mainly inhabited this planet now crossed her mind. She felt discouraged for a moment. But then her indomitable will got the upperhand; she was obsessed by a fanatical desire to carry out her plan and to show Rhodan that she was

59

superior and independent of him. No wild animals would deter her from her decision.

She cast a last glance through the cabin window, then swiftly manipulated the mechanism to open the emergency exit. The door seemed to be stuck but R-17 leaned heavily against the resisting door and it opened suddenly with a shrill squeaky noise. The sultry Venusian atmosphere quickly penetrated the cabin, bringing with it the smells of nature – soil, plants, life.

R-17 was the first to climb down the narrow ladder; he stood waiting on the hard, dry soil. His artificial eyes pierced the darkness and he saw everything as if the sun were shining and illuminating the entire landscape with broad daylight.

This of course was not known to Rabow and his men. Under cover of darkness they crept toward the wrecked spaceship like a hunter stalking his prey. They had no idea who the occupants of the craft might be. They could just as likely be members of the Western Bloc as of the Asiatic Federation. Bright light came from the cabin window. They could make out the shadows of two people. Then the door sprang open and two figures left the ship, or whatever remained of it.

The light in the cabin remained burning; the two people had not even bothered switching it off.

Sgt Rabow gave a signal to his companions. The three men firmly gripped their weapons and tried to see through the darkness. The light in the ship's cabin served them as a point of reference but they could not catch a glimpse of the two people that had just left it. Perhaps they were still standing right next to the ship, for Rabow could not detect the slightest movement.

R-17, unperturbed as ever, spoke to Thora: 'We are most fortunate – there are some human beings ahead. I can see them very clearly. Four armed men. They were coming nearer. If I wanted to I could easily kill them.'

Thora quickly overcame her surprise. 'No, don't. Why kill them? Are they enemies?'

'Quite possibly, judging by their approach to this wreck. They are trying to conceal their presence, this would definitely not indicate peaceful intentions. They saw the spaceship crash. Now they are coming in search of booty. Maybe they were the ones who shot us down.'

'R-17, you know as well as I that we were shot down by the station's electronic guard system,' reprimanded Thora. 'Who are these four men? Can you recognize any more details?'

'They look as if they had been living in this jungle for many years.'

Immediately all was clear to Thora: they must belong to the lost space landing mission of the Eastern Bloc. And that spelled danger! Potential enemies.

Should this still hold true here in the wilderness where each depended on his fellow man?

She shrugged her shoulders. 'They may not be very friendly disposed towards us, R-17, but we should first find out what they want from us. Be on the alert and intervene at once, if necessary. Let them come close to us. I want to talk to them. They don't know that you can see them in the dark.'

R-17 and Thora waited in silence until Rabow and his men were within a few feet of them. Then Thora started to address them in English, the earth tongue she was most familiar with. 'What do you want here?'

The sergeant was thunderstruck when he suddenly heard a female voice talking to him in the darkness. He was so startled that he stumbled, lost his balance and fell face down onto the ground. His weapon flew out of his belt and crashed noisily into a nearby rock. He uttered a florid Russian curse, a stream of the most colorful expletives.

Rabow was still stretched out on the ground. He said: 'We have come to help you. Who are you?'

R-17, who could see the sergeant very clearly, answered: 'We would appreciate any assistance. I assume you belong to General Tomisenkow's troops.'

Rabow had painfully scrambled to his feet meanwhile. The man's voice sounded so strange. Harsh, almost mechanical, he thought, even if his English was perfect. The sergeant knew English very well. So, these must be people from the Western Bloc who had been shot down here.

'Yes, we are Tomisenkow's men.'

'We must stick together if we want to survive in this wilderness,' stated Thora. 'How did you manage to find us so fast?'

Rabow had come closer and now stood in the light coming from the cabin. His disheveled appearance did not make a very confidence inspiring impression. Fear befell Thora as she imagined what might happen if she were to fall into the hands of these ruffians. But she quickly comforted herself with the thought that she had R-17 with her to protect her.

The first few moments, Rabow did not pay too much attention to Thora's whitish hair and reddish albino eyes. He saw only the woman in her. It had been many months for him and the rest of his companions that he had not laid eyes on any female human being. He was a rough and brave man but the unaccustomed sight made him feel embarrassed. He shifted from one foot to the other and finally stammered: 'We saw your ship crash. Our camp is close by. General Tomisenkow sent us to find you.'

'Then take us to him. We must talk to him.' Thora felt

quite confident now. She had quickly sized up the situation.

Rabow eagerly nodded his head. But then he remembered that there was some urgent information he had to obtain first from the two people here. 'Are you the only two who survived the crash?'

'We were the only passengers on this ship; nobody besides the two of us,' replied Thora, paying no attention to Rabow's obvious surprise. 'Let's go. I don't feel like standing around here all night long.'

It dawned on Sgt Rabow that he and the strange woman had somehow changed positions: she, the prisoner, was giving orders to him now. But instinctively he wanted to avoid alienating her. He commanded his three men to return to camp and to sling their rifles back onto their shoulders. While the others were marching ahead he himself preferred walking beside Thora. He hardly paid any more attention to the other survivor. Out of sheer politeness he inquired of R-17, who had kept himself in the dark background: 'I hope you didn't get injured during the crash.'

The robot stated truthfully in a precise voice: 'Only a cable became detached. It was easy to repair. Unfortunately the same is not true of the ship. I'm afraid it is beyond repair.'

It took several seconds before Sgt Rabow became aware that this answer did not seem to make sense. 'A cable?' he mumbled, perplexed. 'Where did a cable become detached?'

'Inside my body, didn't I just tell you?'

Rabow stopped in his tracks. R-17 did not react fast enough and ran into him. Rabow staggered under the impact; it felt as if a light armored tank had run into him. Instinctively he grabbed Thora's arm; she fortunately steadied herself against a tree trunk.

R-17's left arm was raised in a threatening manner.

'Who are you?' stammered Rabow, completely baffled.

Thora freed herself from the sergeant's grip. She was quite annoyed. 'Don't be so impulsive, my good man. My companion is a robot. Is there anything so special about this?'

Rabow naturally had never before run into any robots but he knew that the only people on Earth who possessed them were Rhodan and his New Power. How then could the Western Bloc have laid hands on this robot? Or – a new thought flashed through his mind – what if these two did *not* belong to the Western Bloc? But if so why had they been shot down by their own station?

Something did not seem quite right here. He decided to put a direct question to the strange woman. 'Are you part of the New Power?'

'Did you ever doubt it?' replied Thora with an impatient gesture of her hand which only could be seen by R-17. 'Do you intend to stay here forever?'

Rabow cast a furtive glance in the direction where he presumed the robot to be standing and waiting for them to continue on their way. He started to move forward again.

A woman and a robot . . .

The strangest catch he or Gen Tomisenkow had ever made in their whole life!

Son Okura was awakened by a noise. At first he could not tell what exactly that noise had been and what might have caused it. It took even several long seconds before he could remember where he was.

Yes, that was it – he together with Perry Rhodan and John Marshall were sitting on a broad tree branch some 10 yards above the ground in the middle of the jungle of the virgin planet. It was pitch dark. Somewhere ahead of them to the West was the station of the Arkonides on the high plateau of a mountain. Somewhere behind them to the East was the wreckage of their burnt-out spacecraft.

There was that noise again.

Okura's legs were hurting but he paid no attention to the pain now. He had more important things to do. He activated the mutated part of his brain – and the night turned suddenly into day for him. He could see in the dark.

Rhodan was two yards away from him, half sitting, half lying, his back supported by a thinner branch. Next to him Marshall squatted on the broad branch, his mouth half-way open, snoring loudly. No, that wasn't the sound that had startled him from his sleep. Marshall had his right hand in his pocket; Okura could have bet his meager water ration that John's hand was firmly gripping his trusty old-fashioned revolver even in his sleep.

It was a dragging noise; it came from the left where the giant trunk of the tree reared up to the canopy of the primeval forest, more than 300 feet above the ground.

Okura sat; he did not move at all. He tried to recognize what might cause this noise. And when he recognized it, his heart almost stopped, but then the blood began to rush so to his head that it felt like bursting.

Slowly the yellow 'it' pushed along the trunk, then advanced across the fork where the side branch that the three men were sitting on branched off. 'It' advanced toward them with even vertical waves of its body.

Never before in his life had Okura caught sight of a Venusian snail-worm. Most likely no man alive had ever beheld this creature. It was living deep in the midst of the immense primeval forests, hiding itself during the day in hollowed out tree trunks from which it emerged only at night. It nourished itself by a variety of organic materials – plants, soft wood and meat. Anything that moved either slowly or not at all fell victim to its ravenous appetite.

The snail-worm could not be classified as a beast of prey that ran and jumped in pursuit of its victims.

But just looking at it was sufficient to cause Okura to grow stiff with fright. He seemed paralyzed with fear. He simply stared at the horrifying creature as it slowly crept toward him. The monstrosity reminded him of a snail, at least its head. It extended long feelers that kept vibrating and groping for any obstacle. At the end of these feelers were small eyes. The rest of the beast's body was in the shape of a worm. A long, flexible body without any legs but with innumerable annulations which permitted the animal to advance in vertical half-looped movements.

The most frightening part was the creature's voracious mouth with *three* staggered rows of teeth. These pointed, needle-like extrusions could crush anything that had the misfortune to be seized by them. Certainly including bones!

Okura had come thus far in his deliberations when the creature suddenly stopped. Its long stalked eyes pointed in the direction of the Japanese as if it could perceive him in the dark. It probably could actually see in the absence of visible light. Anyhow it seemed to have caught scent of its prey and perhaps was wondering if it would be slow enough that it could no longer escape.

Okura saw that the worm measured at least five yards in length. He could easily picture its insides as offering sufficient space to accommodate him as well as at least one more of his companions, particularly when it would first have mashed them down with its ferocious teeth. The unpleasant prospect of becoming a tasty meal for this beast revived him from his paralysis and his strength returned.

Quickly he pulled his raygun from his belt and released the safety catch. He made sure first that the control lamp glowed red, which told him that the energy remaining in his weapon would be enough to finish off 10 of these horrible snaky beasts. As soon as Okura felt the weapon in his hand the last remains of his fear dissipated, the terror that had rendered him temporarily powerless to act. No creature alive on this planet would be able to resist the pulse-ray gun of the Arkonides.

The snail-worm must have decided it worth a try to get closer to its intended prey. The annulated sections of its body started to move again and the creeping noise that had awakened Okura a short while before could be heard again. The Japanese looked questioningly at his sleeping companions, then shrugged his shoulders. He hoped they would not fall off their perch high up in the tree when the hissing of the discharging gun would jolt them from their well-deserved slumber.

He took careful aim, which was not too difficult even for someone with such poor eyesight as Okura, considering the small distance that separated the worm from him. He pushed down on the firing button. The thin energy beam hit the beast right in its head. The feelers, the eyes, the voracious mouth and the upper part of its body vaporized and vanished in the energy flames that flared up instantaneously. The rest of the snail-worm reared up wildly, slid sideways over the branch and dropped to the ground. A dull thud told Okura of its fate.

Rhodan was wide awake immediately. He sat up and saw how Okura stamped out the small flames before they could reach the dried leaves and creeper plants. 'What's going on here, Okura?'

'Some kind of a snake. It was creeping up on us but I woke up in time. It wouldn't be a bad idea to start up again.'

Marshall turned over on his side. 'What's all the noise?' he complained, still half asleep. 'It's still pitch dark. I want to sleep; I'm dead tired.'

'You'd soon have been just plain - dead,' explained Rhodan calmly. 'If Okura had not waked up in time we would have been devoured by now by . . .'

'By – what?' Marshall was still far too sleepy to undertake probing Okura's mind to find out the true state of affairs.

'Some kind of a monster. Sort of like a snake. Okura caught sight of it just in time and killed it. Didn't you hear all the commotion?'

Marshall was now sitting next to Rhodan. He shook his head. 'How could I have heard anything? You know I was asleep.'

This sounded like a logical explanation. Marshall set about preparing their breakfast. The spot where the snail-worm had so recently expired was still glowing and provided some light while he was working.

Half an hour later they were marching through the jungle again. Okura walked ahead, the raygun in his hand, ready to shoot if necessary. His eyes kept probing the darkness for any lurking dangers. The soil was still dry. But as their path seemed to lead them imperceptibly but constantly downhill, they could easily figure out that it would not be long until they would stumble on some swamp. All three men were quite worried by this prospect.

Somewhere off to their right a slight rustling could be heard. Marshall, who brought up the rear of the little column, raised his gun but naturally could not find his aim in the darkness. He heard the footsteps of some creature that was stomping through the dense thicket not 10 yards off to the side. There was a slight pressure in his brain. 'Somebody' was thinking. Without expecting too much, he decided to activate his telepathic receiving area – and used his ESP powers.

And sure enough, he received the thoughts of the un-known being. The thoughts were very primitive and super-ficial, mainly concerned with prey and food, but still, de-finite thought impulses.

'There is somebody over to the right,' he whispered just loud enough for Rhodan's and Okura's ears. 'Can you see him?'

The Japanese turned his head over to the right and nodded. 'It's that gorilla-like shadow again; we already noticed it yesterday. Some kind of a big ape. As long as he doesn't attack us we don't need to worry about him. Strange that he doesn't pay attention to us. He must have noticed us by now.'

'Maybe he takes us for fellow apes,' murmured Rhodan. His thoughts were now much more preoccupied with the 300 mile hike that lay ahead of them. He was cursing him-self more and more for having taken off after Thora so rashly and ill-prepared. Why had he not pursued her with a thoroughly tested and dependable ship?

They no longer paid any heed to their invisible com-panion but concentrated on making as much headway as they could, until they reached the shore of a small lake. There they stopped for a rest period. A distant dull roar came from farther ahead in the darkness. Rhodan asked

Okura if he could recognize where this noise was coming from.

'I am not quite sure,' replied the Japanese, 'but as far as I can make out there is a narrow valley with a few smaller swamps and a river. There is a mountain beyond that. I can see big waterfalls. Up above on the plateau the forest is not so dense. It will be much easier for us to march through it. We should make good time up there.'

They lit a camp fire. The ground was damp but there was plenty of dry wood a few feet above in the trees. The flames were flickering brightly, casting grotesque shadows against the dark nocturnal background. Okura kept scanning the area around their camp but he need not have worried: the Venusian animals knew fire only in the form of erupting volcanoes – and stayed away from it.

The water of the lake was not fit to drink, even when they tried to boil it. Marshall cooked their meal and remarked that they would soon be forced to hunt for food if they did not want to starve. Rhodan reassured him that things would improve once they reached the waterfalls and the long night was over.

Shortly before midnight they arrived at the steep rock wall. The sun would rise in about 60 hours; they could not wait until then. During their march through the lowlands beyond the lake, Okura had shot a small animal with Marshall's revolver. This provided plenty of food for the next few meals. And now as they were standing before the rock wall the distant roar had finally grown to a thundering rumble from a huge nearby waterfall whose waters rushed earthwards from a great height.

'We'll make camp here and get a good rest,' declared Rhodan. 'Let's build a fire and erect a wall from some of these boulders. That should provide us enough protection against any marauding animals. Afterwards we'll climb up the wall to get to the plateau.'

Okura glanced up into the eternal dark of the Venusian night. It had cooled off considerably, although it was still much warmer than a summer night on Earth.

'The plateau lies a good 300 yards above the plain down here,' he stated. 'But I can't see how we can climb up there.'

'And we have no ropes,' added Marshall.

Rhodan brushed off the objections of his companions. 'We have no alternative. Besides, just remember, once we reach the mesa above it will be so much easier and simpler to march across it than continuing on our way down below in the tricky swamps and the dangerous jungle. If ever there are human settlers on Venus they'll have to live on these rocky island plateaus. But now we should forget all that and concentrate on getting a hot meal ready. Let's start a fire, Marshall, and you, Okura, skin and clean that deer you shot.'

By the light of their camp fire they saw that the animal they had bagged bore little resemblance to a deer. Though it had no more than four legs, still they were so short that Okura began to believe that he had caught a largish dachshund. It had the same pointed, narrow muzzle, rather long, floppy ears. Its tail was completely missing and instead of fur it was covered by smooth, slippery skin.

'Looks like a well-shaved wart-hog,' grumbled Marshall, but licked his lips in anticipation. 'I am a great lover of animals but I wouldn't care to have that as my pet.'

'Nothing like a good roast,' said Rhodan; 'it beats those concentrates any time.' He kept watching interestedly as Okura carved up the animal.

Two hours later, their stomachs pleasantly filled, they leaned against the rock wall that had been warmed by their fire. 'Splendid!' Marshall praised his own culinary efforts.

71

'It could have used some salt,' murmured Rhodan, feeling very drowsy from the food and the fire.

'Let's call it a dachs-hog,' suggested a sleepy Okura.

Nobody talked for a while. Suddenly their silence was rent by a rifle shot.

Hearing a gun fired on this deserted planet was so incongruous and surprising a sound for the three men that this fact did not immediately register on their brains. Marshall just kept staring into the flames, lost in his thoughts. It would have been most interesting for an uninvolved observer to experience his reaction vicariously.

Marshall nodded his head several times, listened attentively and then said: 'Sounds as if somebody was hunting a dachs-hog and got it with the first shot. Direct hit.' He poked around in the burning logs, noticed the wide open eyes of the two other men. He turned as white as a sheet. 'Good Lord! *Sombody fired a gun!*'

Okura leapt to his feet. 'That's impossible! Who could have?'

Rhodan was just as dumbfounded as the two others but his brain worked faster and more logically. In a fraction of a second he had registered the fact that a shot had been fired, concluded that this must have been done by a human being, determined that there must be people on Venus and knew at once who they were. Of course, he remembered the geographical location where Gen Tomisenkow's troops had landed and subsequently had been defeated by him, at the same time he was aware of their own position on the planet's surface and arrived at the same conclusion:

The lost space troops of the Eastern Bloc must be dwelling on this plateau.

He looked over to Okura. 'Why should it be impossible? We are not the only human beings on Venus. Besides – it might have been Thora, couldn't it?'

'Thora the Arkonide would never bother with terrestrial shotguns,' remarked the Japanese doubtfully.

'That leaves Tomisenkow's men,' said Rhodan.

'From the Eastern Bloc?' Marshall was still not quite with it. 'What would they be doing here?'

'Hunting.'

Their conversation was interrupted. Another shot, quickly followed by a round of gunfire. From another direction came the reply, irregular rifle shots. It was quite obvious now there must be two hostile groups facing each other and shooting at each other. This, of course, changed the whole situation; they would have to readjust their plans.

'I don't think it's advisable to try joining them,' remarked Rhodan to his companions. 'They'd recognize me and I wouldn't live another five minutes. After all, I am the one that put them in this predicament here on Venus – at least that's what they believe. On the other hand, they have rifles, much better for hunting game than your revolver, Marshall. I suggest one of us will have to get in touch with them.'

'Quite risky,' said Okura. 'But I'd be willing to do it, especially since I can see them before they could see me.'

'True, but only at night. I think we'd better make the climb up the rock wall together and then decide how to proceed from there.'

There was still occasional gunfire while they packed up their gear, wrapped the rest of the meat in big leaves and stored it in a container, refilled their water supply, then banked the fire.

'Couldn't we get a few more hours' sleep before we start out again?' inquired Marshall. 'We aren't in such a rush, are we?'

Rhodan listened for a few minutes. Things had quieted down up on the plateau. 'We'll break camp in five hours.

That will give us enough time to refresh ourselves. Sure, we are not missing anything, if we wait a little longer. I can't figure out why they are shooting each other. What could they be fighting about?'

Okura stretched out underneath a rocky outcrop that provided a roof-like shelter. 'About Venus, what else? And judging by what I know of these guys, they probably are at loggerheads because they can't agree on the form the future organization of Venusian society should have.'

'You might be right, Okura,' said Rhodan seriously, 'but they are quarreling there about something they'll never have to make a decision on anyhow.'

'Most people do that,' said Marshall angrily and closed his eyes. Judging by his expression he was far more interested now in dreaming of tasty dachs-hog chops than reflecting about political nonsense.

The fire died down and it became dark again.

And it remained dark until a sudden bright light rent the inky night. But this took place only a few hours later.

Sgt Rabow had handed over Thora and the robot at Gen Tomisenkow's 'headquarters.' He was secretly surprised at the deep satisfaction of his commander-in-chief. Then he had left for patrol duty in the company of 20 men. Their mission was to scout out the rebels' rocky plateau and – if possible – to take some prisoners. Gen Tomisenkow wanted to find out if the rebels were planning an attack against him and his forces.

It was a long march through the swamps, lowlands and jungle, but he had been on this road many a time. He knew the markings which led to the rock island of the 'enemy' and some day he was determined to go this way all by himself, straight to the enemy's camp – whenever he felt the time would be ripe.

But that time had not yet come; it was still too soon.

Rabow's patrol was not the only one out that night. A small army of at least 200 men also approached the rebels' plateau but from the opposite direction. They belonged to another group of former members of Tomisenkow's invasion forces and had struck out on their own as well. They did not wish to be part of either Tomisenkow's or the rebels' camp, because of their outlook on life. They called themselves totalitarian pacifists and they were determined to bring the rebels over to their side – even by force if necessary. Their leader was a certain Lt Wallerinski.

Wallerinski's group was the first to reach the rebels' island plateau. He and his men climbed up the sheer wall and took the sentries by surprise. True to his pacifist principles he did not kill the guards but took them prisoner in order to put them through a third degree interrogation. This way he learned the location of the rebels' hiding place.

One hour later, Wallerinski and his men came upon the outpost of the rebels. The guard was wide awake, as he should be, and succeeded in firing a warning shot which aroused the entire camp. Ten minutes later the two groups were embroiled in a bitter gun fight.

Rabow and his men were still several miles away from the rebels' island plateau when they heard the shooting. They stopped to hold a brief council of war and arrived at the conclusion that there must be further units of scattered troops in the vicinity who made each other's life miserable.

He was just about to give an order to resume marching when one of his men came running toward him in great excitement. 'Light!' he shouted breathlessly. 'There's a fire at the edge of the plateau. I can see it quite clearly.'

'Where? At the bottom of the plateau?'

'Yes, at the foot of the cliff. Maybe another outpost of the rebels?'

'Sure, you idiot,' mocked Rabow, 'so they can be seen

for miles around!' He had some idea who it might be but if he had really known he would have thought twice before issuing the order 'Let's have a look and find out!'

And thus, two hours later, he looked down upon the three sleeping men who were rudely awakened by Rabow's bright searchlight.

As these three men looked well-kempt and neither wore the uniform of Gen Tomisenkow's former dispersed forces, Rabow addressed them in English. He was convinced now that the woman whose spaceship had been shot down had been lying. She had *not* arrived all alone, as she had pretended.

'Keep your hands off your guns,' he warned them. 'Twenty rifles are pointing at you. One of my men will come to get your weapons.'

Perry Rhodan was furious. What a fatal mistake! One should never lie down and sleep in an area where shooting was going on. Now they would have to pay for their carelessness. He whispered softly to Okura: 'Can you see anything?'

The Japanese whispered back: 'He isn't lying. They have surrounded us and all their rifles are pointed at us. We could eliminate a few of them . . .'

'What are our chances?'

'Oh, we are outnumbered by about 10 to one.'

'That's too risky,' whispered Rhodan. Then he called out aloud: 'Send your man to get our guns! Who are you?'

'You'll find out in due time. Were you involved in that shooting some time ago?'

'If you are referring to that gun battle, I'll have to disappoint you. That was higher up there on the plateau.'

Rhodan offered no resistance when Rabow's man pulled the raygun from his belt. He noted with satisfaction that Marshall had kept his trusty old revolver hidden deep in his pocket. Okura did not look too happy when his weapon was taken away from him. The smile had vanished from his face for the first time.

'Well,' said the man behind the searchlight, 'now that's done we can have a chat.'

With these words he stepped from the darkness into the light. Rhodan could finally see the man who had outwitted him. Not a very encouraging sight, he thought, and hoped that the man would not recognize him. The thought of having fallen into the hands of those men he had for all practical purposes left stranded in the Venusian wilderness, was none too pleasant.

'I am Sgt Rabow of Gen Tomisenkow's army,' Rabow introduced himself. 'And who are you?'

That was a 64,000 dollar question which required a precise answer. At least an answer, decided Rhodan, that sounded as clear as possible. 'I am part of an expedition,' he started cautiously, 'which was sent here to test the alertness of Rhodan's Venusian fortress.'

'Who sent you?'

'Who do you think?' stalled Rhodan.

'The Americans?'

'Possibly.'

Rabow interpreted this as an affirmative reply. He was only baffled why the girl should have been lying earlier and why these three men should have deserted her and the robot.

'You are all alone here I presume. Had a crash landing?'

'You guessed right.'

'Hm!' Rabow pondered for a while. He did not want to lay all his cards on the table. His prisoners need not find out from him that he had already found the other survivors from the wrecked spaceship. He remembered some old saying, that it was always best to leave your adversary in the dark about his situation. In any case, it was interesting that this man admitted belonging to the Western Bloc while the woman had asserted she represented the New Power. 'And where did your spaceship come down?'

Rhodan pointed toward the East. 'Over there in the Jungle. We were shot down.'

This answer did not impress Rabow as quite plausible. 'You mean you were shot down over the jungle and not over a plateau? And after your crash landing you walked all this way to here?'

'Yes. Does that sound so strange?'

Rabow did not reply. He was facing a difficult decision. Should he bring these prisoners back to Gen Tomisenkow's camp or should he hand them over – as a token of good will – to the rebels which he intended to join? And finally there was still another unsolved problem: who and what was that third group that had attacked the rebels a little while ago? Perhaps it would be wiser to wait until it would be clear who had won that battle?

The last solution seemed to make most sense to him.

'You'll come with us,' he said to Rhodan. 'Let's go, men, and find out what has happened up there. Who knows, we might be the third party here and have the laugh on our side.'

The climb turned out to be wearisome and not without danger. Several of Rabow's men took over the lead; they knew the secret path well enough to be able to find it even in the dark. Rhodan, Marshall and Okura came next, followed directly by Rabow. The rest of the soldiers of Rabow's patrol brought up the rear.

Seven hours later they came to a halt for a short rest period. Rabow explained that it would not take much longer now. Rhodan was quite surprised at his behavior. Rabow was reserved and discreet, almost polite. Rhodan had expected to be treated quite differently by his captor. Even assuming that Rabow had not recognized him, it was

78

amazing how considerate he was of his three prisoners' well-being. Rhodan made a mental note of it; he decided not to forget this.

Marshall was sitting next to Rhodan. It was obvious that he was impatient to communicate something to Rhodan. But Rabow's presence held him back. He had to postpone whatever he had in mind and wait for a better opportunity.

The party resumed its march after 10 minutes' rest and half an hour later they arrived at the plateau. Once again shots could be heard coming from a distance. Okura was walking beside Rhodan now and at the first opportunity he whispered to him: 'Shall I escape? It's easy.'

That seemed a very plausible suggestion. The Japanese could see clearly in the dark night. Also their captors had refrained from handcuffing them. If Okura remained close by he could always intervene if ever the situation should become critical.

Rabow had noticed the whispering going on between the two and warned them politely: 'I prefer if you remain silent.'

Rhodan simply nodded his consent to Okura while he spoke to Rabow: 'Don't worry, I am staying with you quite voluntarily. How else could I manage all alone in that wilderness? I am relying on your help to get me out of here.'

This seemed to reassure Rabow.

They reached a turn in the narrow path and suddenly Okura vanished. Nobody except Rhodan noticed Okura's flight for everyone was far too preoccupied with their own safety, trying to avoid fallen tree trunks and loose boulders and pebbles underfoot. The distant shots had come closer. The battle was still going on apparently.

The terrain was not quite so rough now. Way ahead the area was all lit up, as if a fire had broken out in the forest. Probably the rebel settlement too had been set afire.

79

Volleys of shots rang out through the night. In between came detonations of smaller grenades, punctuated by the dull boom of larger cannons.

Rhodan was pleased to note that no atomic weapons were being deployed. The future settlers of Venus had not yet reached that advanced stage of 'civilization' where they made use of the latest accomplishments of human technology.

By now the bullets were whizzing around their ears; all threw themselves on the ground to take cover. Rabow was stretched out next to Rhodan, whom he had not let out of sight for a single moment. The little village of the colonists, that was burning brightly beyond the next little forest, gave sufficient light to see things quite clearly now. There were only occasional trees that offered little cover.

'Where is your Japanese?' panted Rabow and nervously fingered his heavy pistol. 'I hope he didn't . . . ?'

'He is in the vicinity,' declared Rhodan quite truthfully. 'Maybe he wants to reconnoitre things a bit more. And quite frankly, I don't consider myself actually your prisoner. Let's be reasonable, Rabow – that's your name, isn't it? – we are confronted here by a common enemy. We should therefore make a common cause, before they force us to do so.'

'My orders were not to make contact with the enemy, only to scout out the situation. I must know who attacked the village of the rebels.'

'Rebels?' wondered Rhodan.

'They rebelled against Gen Tomisenkow and decided to to remain here voluntarily on Venus in order to establish a colony.'

'What else should they have done? Didn't Gen Tomisenkow agree to this solution?'

'The general is determined to carry out his orders to take Rhodan's fortress here on Venus.'

Rhodan shook his head. 'That's sheer nonsense. He doesn't have a ghost of a chance. Back on Earth there is already peace between Rhodan and the Eastern Bloc. Tomisenkow's army is considered to be a total loss.'

Rabow did not say anything. So, the rebels were right after all when they decided to make a fresh start here on Venus! Why not? Why shouldn't they begin a new life here on a new world? But who were these people that had attacked the rebel camp? Another group that had split off from Tomisenkow's forces and that they had not known about all this time?

Now he made up his mind to place his cards on the table. 'I do not know who you are. But one thing is clear to me: you have lied to me. You do not belong to the Western Bloc but are part of Rhodan's New Power. Why did you conceal this from me?'

'What gives you that idea?'

'I just know it. The only thing that puzzles me is why your ship was shot down by Rhodan's guns? Do you have anything against Rhodan?'

'Not against him personally,' said Rhodan with self derision, 'only against his occasional lapses of carelessness.'

'I can't understand that.' Rabow shook his head and looked ahead where the flash of a detonation momentarily lit up the landscape as light as day. Sporadic shooting was now quite close. The sound of hurrying steps and trampling came from the pebble-strewn slopes. The outlines of running men were etched like dark shadows against the burning horizon.

'How do you know that I belong to the New Power?' asked Rhodan while looking at Marshall at the same time.

Before Rabow could reply the telepath supplied an answer to Rhodan's mute question. 'A spaceship was shot down over on the other rock plateau. Rabow found in it a woman and a robot. Both are now in the hands of Gen Tomisenkow.'

Marshall did not mention the woman's name on purpose but Rhodan knew immediately that Thora had not reached the Venus fortress and that she, too, had been shot down. How fortunate that she had survived the crash. She must have told her captors who she was. This fact certainly wouldn't help things as Tomisenkow was bound to hold on to this prize at all costs.

'Is that the truth?' he asked Rabow.

The sergeant nodded, perplexed. 'How can he know about it?'

Perry Rhodan did not react to his question. 'Who is that woman?' he inquired.

'She didn't give us her name, she only said she was a member of the New Power. But she did lie when she told us she had come with just one companion, the robot. You came with her; why did you separate? Why?'

Rhodan realized it would be advantageous if they did not connect him in any way with Thora's flight. There was a chance then that they would not recognize his identity. On the other hand, Tomisenkow had no idea that Thora had fled and was being pursued. And he was bound before long to recognize her as being an alien Arkonide.

What a tricky situation!

But Rhodan had hardly a second to worry about that situation. There was a flash directly in front of his face; his eardrums were deafened by a sudden explosion. Somebody screamed and then collapsed abruptly. There were shadowy figures everywhere all of a sudden, that pounced on the men who had been quietly lying on the ground.

Rhodan noticed that Marshall suddenly jumped up and instantly vanished in the bushes over at the side. He could hear his steps as he hastily ran off but he could not decide to follow him, although the opportunity for escape seemed unique.

The new situation demanded that he stay with Rabow whatever the outcome.

The hand-to-hand fighting was accompanied by screaming and shouting. It became evident to the attackers that they had mistaken Rabow's men for their enemies the rebels. A loud voice commanded Rabow and his men to surrender. They would be permitted to keep their weapons but they were asked to negotiate and confer and not continue this senseless massacre.

That impressed Rabow as a sensible suggestion. He ordered his men to cease fire. All but four obeyed; but these four would never again even hear another command: they were dead.

The unexpected foe, too, had suffered casualties, but in the darkness and in the general confusion it was difficult to assess the damage right away. Rabow stood next to Rhodan. He did not appear to have noticed Marshall's flight, or at least he acted that way. Perhaps he deemed it wiser at this moment not to discuss this matter.

A primitive torch was lit. A tall black-bearded man stepped close to the source of light. He must have recognized Rabow as the leader of this troop because he stopped in front of him.

'Who are you?' he inquired in a domineering voice. 'Do you belong to the rebels?'

'I could ask the same question of you,' countered Rabow. His right hand with his pistol was now dangling down his side. 'You have killed four of my men.'

'So, you are not part of the rebels. Strange. Maybe you belong to Gen Tomisenkow's forces?'

'And if so, what about it?'

'It would be just as bad – at least for you. We don't want

to have any dealings with anybody – neither with Tomisenkow nor his opponents.'

'And why have you attacked the rebels?'

The tall man did not answer that question. Instead he said: 'Follow me to the village. We'll talk more there. Perhaps you'll see the light, then we can arrange matters. The survivors of the rebels have already joined us.'

'And who are you?'

The unknown black-bearded man proudly stuck out his chest. 'I am Wallerinski, the president of the pacifists.'

Rabow nodded his head; he understood. Then he winked at Rhodan and pointed at the four dead soldiers who had become victims of a recent attack.

'I see,' sighed Rabow, 'you are pacifists. It's always the same, even here on Venus. The same masquerade of mankind's dogmas. Everything is turned around and masked under borrowed cloaks. Pacifists murder and burn down a village. Rebels have settled peacefully on the land and are now being chased away from their property. Regular armed forces lead a life of robber barons. Truly, everything is all mixed up, a topsy-turvy world.'

'What do you mean by that?' growled Wallerinski furiously.'

Rabow shrugged his shoulders. 'Just what I said.' But then he added in a more conciliatory tone, 'We'll come along with you. But don't think for a minute that you can treat us as your prisoners.'

Rhodan had to admit to himself that he liked Sgt Rabow.

Okura, who had all the time stayed close to the patrol, observed the attack and the surprising truce that quickly followed. He saw also Marshall's escape and made sure that they would both link up again shortly. Together they followed Rabow's and Wallerinski's men, who were eyeing each other with distrust all along the march toward the village.

'We ought to rescue Rhodan,' murmured Okura. He felt ill at ease that the man he so admired was still in the hands of the enemy. But Marshall shook his head. 'He would not agree to that. I can now very well receive his thoughts; among other thoughts he is also sending messages to me. He plans to remain with Rabow, for he is the only one who can lead him to Thora. He is in no danger for the time being. If matters get sticky we are to rescue him and Rabow, but if possible without any bloodshed.'

'Let's hope we notice in time when the situation gets critical.' The Japanese remained skeptical. 'I don't like that blackbearded guy.'

'Wallerinski? A harmless fanatic.'

'Are there any harmless fanatics?' doubted Okura. 'Even the most stupid fanatic can be dangerous. I wonder what Wallerinski is so fanatic about?'

'He is fanatic about his cause, pacifism,' answered Marshall somberly. 'Tell me what can you see now?'

'There is a village ahead. It's half burned down. The inhabitants have fled. The work of a pacifist if you are right.'

Okura's words sounded bitter. He knew how much mischief had been committed in the name of 'pacifism.' It was the fashion nowadays to hide aggressive actions under the cloak of pacifism and to pretend that these war-like acts served the cause of peace. Thank God things had changed since Perry Rhodan's New Power had come into existence. But here on Venus the history of mankind stood only at the beginning.

At the edge of the clearing, Okura and Marshall came to a halt. They did not dare to advance out into the open. But though Okura lost visual contact with Rhodan, Marshall still kept in touch with him. It was only a one-way communication. Rhodan was unfortunately only a very weak telepath but he knew that his thoughts would be received by Marshall. And thus it was possible that the Australian Marshall was at all times well-informed about what was going on in the village, even if Rhodan could not use his wristband transmitter to send or receive messages.

In a large assembly hall which was filled with men and occasionally women of the rebel camp, Wallerinski motioned to his men. Then he climbed up on a table, raised both hands and demanded everyone be silent. He glanced swiftly at a group of prisoners in the background, made sure that the exits were guarded by his own soldiers. Then he started to speak.

'Comrades!' he called out in a dominating, none too pleasant sounding voice. 'The fight is over and we have decided to continue on our way together. We want peace on Venus but this can not come about until we have removed the last and greatest threat to peace. This danger is embodied in the person of Gen Tomisenkow. His plan to attack Rhodan's station here on Venus is suicidal. This was the reason we split off from him. You went your separate ways so that you could become peaceful settlers and work toward a better life for yourself. We want the same, a good life. But before we can devote ourselves fully to this task we must first remove Tomisenkow and convince his people of our superior goals. We need a leader for this enterprise.'

Somebody shouted from the door in the back: 'Wallerinski! Wallerinski is our leader! He will bring us liberty and peace!'

Rhodan whispered softly so that only Rabow who was standing beside him could hear his words: 'This is the way all wars have begun. In the name of freedom.'

The sergeant did not reply. He felt vaguely that he was at the threshold of a new decision.

But he had no idea yet what that decision would be.

MULTIPLE MOTIVATIONS

Until further notice Perry Rhodan's mutant corps was under the command of Reginald Bell, the Minister of Security. After atomic bombs were 'born,' certain changes occurred in the genes of certain people exposed to their radiations. Gradually the mutants became known:

There were telepaths who could read the thoughts of others; cephalopaths who psyched brainwave patterns and emotional states; telekineticists capable of moving objects over broad distances by exercizing their will power; teleporters who could transport their own bodies by simply dematerializing and rematerializing at some other place.

There were also the audiopaths, the listeners; and the radiopaths, receiving and hearing radio waves via some special sense.

And, finally, the hypnopaths, who could influence other people's minds even against their will.

The only extra-terrestrial member of the mutant corps was Pucky, the mouse-beaver from the planet Vagabond. While the *Stardust*, the superspaceship of the New Power, had landed for a temporary stay on Vagabond, the hardly one-yard-tall creature had smuggled himself aboard the ship. From that moment on, the little stowaway became a member of Rhodan's close circle of friends.

Despite his appearance, Pucky was not an animal. He was capable of rational thought and was definitely of higher intelligence. Assisted by John Marshall, the little fellow had even learned to speak English, Pankosmo and the Arkonide language. Visitors had often been dumbfounded when the droll little creature would sit down, well-supported by his broad beaver tail, and address them: 'Hello, how are you this fine morning?'

But Pucky's most remarkable talent was telekinesis. He was considered the best 'object-mover' in the entire mutant corps. He had finally been broken of the bad habit of employing this talent at random. It no longer would happen that spaceships suddenly would take off all on their own, or that ray cannons would shoot without being fired by their gunners. In addition he had the gift of telepathy and several other extrasensory perceptional talents which made Pucky a truly universal genius.

Pucky's relationship to Bell consisted mainly in a sort of amicable warfare. This became evident on many occasions. Such as today when Bell summoned the mutant corps to inform them of their imminent mission.

The festivities had come to an end and the world had returned to its daily routine. Bell had given his speech and then devoted his full attention to his work. Rhodan's destroyer had been tracked down by radar and then sighted visually by the New Power's base on the Moon. Then the destroyer had disappeared in the direction of the planet Venus.

Since that time Rhodan seemed to have vanished without a trace. Not a single radio communication from Venus had been received by any of the stations that were on the alert day and night. Bell remembered Rhodan's instruction for any such eventuality. He called the mutants to his office, explained the situation and requested them to assemble in front of the auxiliary vessel *Good Hope V* within half an hour.

The spacesphere had a diameter of 60 yards and could fly faster than light. For ordinary Earthmen this was considered the perfect space vehicle but the Arkonides used it only as an interplanetary 'space shuttle' for their space cruisers of the imperial class.

'Something might have happened to Rhodan,' Bell was finishing his brief address and he concluded with the admonishment: 'I expect you to hurry as fast as you can and report ready for take-off in half an hour. We'll take along 50 fighter robots, besides 10 space fighter planes with pilots. Are there any questions?' Bell looked around. 'None, apparently. Alright, report ready for action in 30 minutes exactly. Dismissed!'

He meant to rush out of the room and almost tripped over Pucky who was waiting for him in the doorway.

'There is something I wanted to ask you,' began the mouse-beaver displaying his lone incisor tooth. Whenever that incisor became visible, people knew that Pucky was grinning. But it did not mean he was in a good humor too. Bell was well aware of that fact – or at least he should have been.

'Go ahead, make it snappy, I'm in a hurry!'

'As a member of the mutant corps am I included in that mission? I just wanted to make sure.'

'You want to go with us to Venus? So you can fool around, create havoc with everything? That's out of the question!'

Bell tried to push past the mouse-beaver but Pucky did not give in so easily. 'I'll complain to Rhodan about it,' he made another attempt.

'You do just that!' growled Bell as he tried in vain to lift his right foot. It was as if it had been nailed to the floor. Some invisible power held it down with an iron grip. Furiously he hissed: 'Stop that nonsense, Pucky! Let go of my foot! That's mutiny!'

'May I go along with you?'

Bell's temper was near exploding. Some of the mutants had stopped and grinned as they watched the word battle between the stocky, red-haired man and the little mouse-beaver. This was more than Bell could bear.

'Of course not!' he decided, although there was still time to avoid an embarrassing contest of wills. He would show that little rodent who was master here! 'This is a job for a man, not a Mickey mouse!'

He should not have said that! Nothing offended Pucky more than being called a Mickey mouse.

Bell felt the pressure leave his foot, then he became as light as a feather. Pucky sat in front of him comfortably supported by his broad tail and regarded him with fascination. His grin grew wider and his incisor gleamed wickedly. His red-brown fur stood on end, forming a curly ruff around his neck.

'Is that final?' Pucky chirped, trembling with excitement. His voice was very high and shrill.

'Yes, final!' shouted Bell at the top of his voice, although he knew full well how senseless it was to contradict Pucky's wishes and what the dire results would be. Even complaining to Rhodan about that saucy little fellow would do no good. He would just laugh at him. Pucky was a special case with special privileges which he exploited to the utmost.

Pucky's eyes, which usually looked soft and mournful like those of a hound dog, changed expression. They assumed a glazed look for an instant as he stared at Bell. But that was caused by his sudden effort at concentration. Now Bell became weightless and rose higher like a balloon. Invisible hands opened the window and Bell began to drift and float outside. There he was hovering, some 90 feet above the asphalt road, nothing between him and the very hard ground below but Pucky's telekinetic forces.

Pucky grinned triumphantly and waddled toward the window. One nimble leap – and he was sitting astride the window sill, contemplating his stubborn friend who stared back at him in helpless rage.

'Well,' squeaked Pucky good-humoredly, 'I am still not

allowed to fly off to Venus with you? You must admit that I can be a most useful ally with unusual talents if I so choose!'

'What good would your telekinetic powers be if you had to lift a prehistoric monster off the ground? I bet you couldn't do it!' snarled Bell while he peered at the void between the bottom of his feet and the street pavement. 'Besides, this is blackmail!'

'What an ugly word!' stated Pucky and suddenly let Bell drop 6 feet. 'I don't like people who use such ugly language.'

'I'd like to do a few much uglier things to you once I can lay my hands on you! Alright, you little monster, I'll consider the matter. Just get me inside again!'

'I want a definite answer. Will you or won't you take me along to Venus?' insisted the little fellow. He seemed to be unaware of the other mutants who followed the spectacle with undivided interest. None of them dared interfere for this might easily have resulted in a catastrophe. If the mouse-beaver should release his telekinetic grip on Bell, the latter risked crashing to the ground. He might break all his bones and his neck as well. But Pucky was not the least concerned; he was most confident of his powers.

Bell eagerly nodded his head to indicate his consent. He tried desperately to reach the wall with his hands. 'Alright, I'll let you go. But under one condition.'

'What would that be?' said Pucky expectantly and let his single tooth disappear.

'You must promise to behave and do whatever I ask you. And no more nonsense until we get back to Earth again!'

The mouse-beaver brought Bell back safely to a soft landing on the window sill. 'It's a deal,' he said magnanimously. 'But if you should break your promise and leave me behind, I'll see to it that you float to the moon without the benefit of a space suit even!'

Bell said not a word as he climbed down from the window sill and walked to the door.

Betty Toufry, the 15-year-old telepathic wonder girl, blushed violently as she together with the other mutants followed Bell with her eyes.

The Minister of Security of the New Power must have *thought* of some juicy but fitting curse words since he no longer dared to voice them out aloud.

Gen Tomisenkow's face bore an expression of deep satisfaction as he contemplated his unexpected guest. What a stroke of good luck! Thora, Rhodan's closest collaborator, had fallen into his hands; the Arkonide woman, to whom Rhodan owed his rise to power.

If he treated her right, some day she might give away some of her secrets to him also. His hopes were not too far-fetched, he thought, for after all it had been Rhodan's own weapons that had shot down Thora's spaceship.

'Most regrettable indeed,' said the general with compassion. 'And you believe it happened by mistake?'

'It was definitely a mistake!' said R-17 with a somewhat creaky voice. His yearly lubricating job must be due by now. The oil in some of the ball bearings of his artificial larynx must have dried up. 'The electronic guard system did not recognize us.'

'Wouldn't it be possible that Rhodan had you shot down on purpose to prevent you from entering the Venus fortress?' asked Tomisenkow with a cunning look.

'Utter nonsense!' replied Thora. 'Rhodan cannot possibly have been here before me.'

'Oh – do you expect him later?'

Thora bit her lip. She kept repeating the same mistake of underestimating these Earthlings. She had almost given herself away. Too late now to pretend that possibility did not exist at all.

'Maybe,' she said; 'anything is possible.' She tried to get off the subject of Rhodan as fast as she could. 'Will you finally let me know why you intend to detain me here? You know as well as I do that my robot could easily destroy your whole encampment. Give me the provisions and the soldiers I asked for – or must I try to reach the station on my own?'

'You would be well-advised not to undertake anything foolish against me and my men. You know you are helpless by yourself. You will never make it alone with your robot to the plateau of the Venus base. It's more than 300 miles from here. You depend on my help and goodwill now. I do not wish to exploit your precarious situation, I want to help you. I'll take you to the station, provided the barrier will let us through.'

'They respond to the wave pattern of Arkonide brains, there is no danger we would be held back by the barrier.'

'Excellent. And once you are standing in front of the station, what will you do next? What will happen to me?'

'You may turn back, nothing untoward will happen to you.'

Gen Tomisenkow grinned cunningly. 'How magnanimous of you, noble Arkonide. Rhodan once saved you on the Moon. You made him a gift in gratitude, you gave him power over our world. I am rescuing you here and you plan to pay me off with a few crumbs. Oh, what am I saying . . . a few crumbs! You want to give me something that is already in my possession. Safety? I have that! No, my dear, if you want to get to the fortress you will pay an acceptable price – or else, you can go it alone.'

He knew that Thora could never manage on her own and he intended to take advantage of that fact. Besides, he was determined to separate her from her robot at the next best opportunity. He planned to take her by surprise. There was no better or more valuable hostage than Thora of Arkon.

Especially if Rhodan should really be on his way to Venus.

Thora clearly sensed the insincerity of the man. She could easily have issued a command to R-17 to annihilate him but would that really be in her own interest? Also, she did not know the kind of arms carried by Tomisenkow's men. There was a chance that they might put R-17 out of commission – and then she would be lost indeed.

'I will accept your offer of help and I understand that I will have to pay for it. Let's wait till morning, then we can decide what we will do next. Till then, please provide some quarters for me and my robot,'

'Does he need to sleep, too?' asked Tomisenkow sarcastically.

Thora shook her head and said in an icy cool voice: 'No, he doesn't need to. But I do.'

Rhodan and Rabow and his men could not be exactly called prisoners. They had been permitted to keep their weapons. Wallerinski had housed them in a large hall with guards placed in front of the entrance 'for their protection.'

Rhodan asked Rabow to return his raygun to him as well as those of his two companions. The sergeant complied with his wish without raising any objections. He seemed to have some idea that he might urgently need the mysterious stranger's help in the near future.

'What do you think will happen next?' inquired Rhodan, who assumed that Rabow was familiar with the mentality of his compatriots. 'Do you think that Wallerinski and his men will really attack the general and his troops?'

'I'm quite sure of that.'

'And don't you believe it is your duty to warn Tomisen-kow?'

Rabow hesitated with his reply. The insurgent group of colonists he had intended to join was practically non-existent by now. He felt no sympathy for Wallerinski, mainly because of his ideology. It would be preferable under the circumstances to throw in his lot again with the General.

'Sure, it would be my duty, but how can I get away from her to warn him?'

'Let me take care of that, don't worry. I wanted to find out your attitude first. My two friends will come and get us. One of them can see by night and can lead us safely through the darkness. Now that I have my weapons back in my possession I could wipe out this whole camp in a few seconds – but what good would it do. . . ?'

Rhodan concentrated his thoughts, hoping that Marshall would receive them now. If so, then he and Okura must already be on their way to the village to rescue him. It might not be a bad idea to leave here and go and meet them.

He turned to Rabow. 'What happened to the woman and her robot who crash landed here before me? Is she safe?'

'Yes, relatively safe,' grinned Rabow. 'But it's been a long time since our men have seen a woman.'

'They sure won't enjoy her company,' prophesied Rhodan grimly. He knew that – if necessary – the robot could change Tomisenkow and his forces into radio-active dust. 'Tell your people here that we'll come later to get them out. Now we can't waste any more time. My friends are already waiting for us. At the edge of the wood, toward the East, if I am not mistaken.'

Rabow issued some commands to his men. Then both he and Rhodan stepped out of the hut into the street. Off to one side was a camp fire with some men sitting around softly talking to each other. Surely they were very tired and would have preferred to go to sleep.

There was nobody stationed directly by their hut.

Rhodan seized Rabow by the hand and relied now more on his instincts than on his eyes. While he made his way toward the East he kept thinking about his location to assist Marshall to find him easier. He fervently hoped that Marshall did not happen to be asleep at that moment!

They soon left the half-burnt down village behind them. It grew darker again the closer they approached the edge of the wood. A light flashed for several seconds. Then Rhodan heard someone walk with a firm step through the underbrush. Nobody could walk that way in the night unless he carried a lantern to light his way.

Okura!

'Yes.' It came like a soft breath of wind blowing gently through the dark till it reached Rhodan's ear. Of course! Okura did not know who his companion was. Marshall must have been lax.

'It's me,' whispered Rhodan. 'Rabow is with me. He'll show us the way to Gen Tomisenkow's camp – and the way to Thora, too.'

Rhodan could feel Rabow give a sudden start.

'The way to whom?' And since he did not get a reply he added: 'Thora – isn't that the Arkonide woman?' And after another small pause he asked: 'And who are you?'

Marshall had joined them. 'Is everything OK?' he inquired and then addressed the sergeant. 'Don't worry, my dear Rabow. You have bet on the right horse here – if you stay with us. Take us to Tomisenkow and let us take care of the rest.'

And thus it came about that three different groups intended paying a visit to the presumably lost general. To be sure, each motivated by very different reasons.

Bell came to look for Rhodan, even though he did not know where to begin the search.

Wallerinski wanted to establish peace by force, even though there was no war.

And finally, Rhodan wanted to free Thora, who, as far as she was concerned, did not wish to be liberated by him. At least not for the time being.

PLANET OF STUBBORN SECRET

This time Reginald Bell abstained from exceeding the speed of light as he took the *Good Hope V* from Earth to Venus. The distance between the two planets was relatively too short to make a jump through hyperspace worthwhile. Earth soon changed into a bright disk; the sun receded into the distance to the left of the auxiliary vessel and then the shiny circle of Venus dominated the section of the sky in front of them.

The auggie – automatic guidance system – was shut off and Bell took charge of navigating the giant space-sphere. He knew exactly the position of the Venus base and had calculated that it was still on the night side of the planet. Sunrise was scheduled in another 40 hours.

Little by little he began to feel uneasy. Supposing all had gone according to plan, then Rhodan should have long since sent some message. Could this mean that he had missed Thora at the Venusian fortress? And if so, what had happened to Thora? She might perhaps have completely foregone touching down on Venus and instead risked an interstellar flight with her destroyer.

Bell depressed the lever of the intercom and established video contact with the ship's radio center. Tanka Seiko was on duty there.

Seiko was of Japanese origin, a high frequency technician by profession and the so called radiopath of the mutant corps. He was capable of receiving directly, without the benefit of any man-made instrument, the radiation of radio stars as well as being able to 'hear' any broadcasts sent by radio stations on Earth, regardless of their wavelengths. There was no man on Earth better equipped to handle the work of the *Good Hope*'s radio communication center.

Seiko's face appeared on the videoscreen. The scar on his right cheek glowed an unnatural red. 'Chief?'

Bell like to be addressed with this title. It was a sign of respect and esteem. Well, after all, he had been officially deputized to take Perry Rhodan's place here as commander-in-chief. This was something to be proud of, indeed.

'Still no news from Rhodan?'

'Total radio silence from Venus,' Seiko said, shaking his head. 'Just as if there was not a single living human being up there.'

'That couldn't be the case. I recall that even the troops of the Eastern Bloc that were lost on Venus had radio equipment with them; they couldn't have lost everything. But I am deeply worried we have not heard from either Rhodan or Thora. It is most peculiar.'

'Their wristband transmitters are too weak for these distances.'

'But not the instruments on the destroyers, Seiko.'

Bell kept racking his brain but he could not find any plausible explanation for this continued radio silence from Venus. Or could Rhodan perhaps. . . ? No, better not think of such a possibility! Maybe the fortress. . . ? But why should it. . . ? Who would dare forbid Rhodan to come in for a landing on Venus? There was no doubt that the positronic guard installation would recognize him as an authorized person.

'Just be on the alert, Seiko. Keep listening. Let me know the moment you hear anything from there. I am now getting ready to come in for a landing.'

The *Good Hope V* descended as far as the upper strata of the cloud cover that eternally enveloped the planet when suddenly the entire spacesphere was violently shaken. Bell was thrown from his chair. While he scrambled to his feet and quickly checked his control panel, the door to the center flew open. Several mutants rushed into the room.

Ralf Marten, the teleoptician, held on to the wall. 'What are you trying to do to us, Reggie? Do you want to kill us all?'

Bell cast a disdainful glance in the direction of the slender dark-haired German-Japanese young man. 'You wouldn't be afraid, would you? But to be quite frank with you, I don't know what happened just now. Wait, will you! There's Seiko.'

Seiko's face was deathly pale as it appeared on the videoscreen. 'There is some news now. From the Venus base. Must be the positronic brain. It refuses to give us permission to land.'

'Wha-a-a-t?' roared Bell. His red, stubby hair began to stand up on his head like the hackles of a fighting cock. His eyes were filled with fury. 'What's the idea? How can that stupid robot dare refuse to give us permission to land? Ask him for his reasons!'

Seiko tried his best but all the time with the same negative result. The radio station of the positronic brain kept sending the identical message with a most enervating stubbornness, regardless of whatever desperate measure the Japanese resorted to:

'SECRET BARRIER X HAS GONE INTO EFFECT. ANY PENETRATION INTO THIS PLANET'S ATMOSPHERE IS BEING REPELLED BY A HYPER-GRAVITATIONAL NEGATIVE FORCE FIELD. REPEAT: SECRET BARRIER X HAS GONE INTO EFFECT...'

The metallic voice went on and on, like a reel on a tape recorder with an endless loop of tape.

Bell finally gave up in sheer disgust. He ordered Seiko to keep listening for other radio communications. Then

Bell switched off the intercom and turned to Marten. 'That indicates that Rhodan could not land either here. The positronic brain must suddenly have gone berserk.'

Bell had no way of knowing that the brain's behavior was merely the logical result of Rhodan's own actions. On the occasion of Rhodan's last stay on Venus he had in person programmed the secret barrier X into the positronic brain.

The brain had been instructed to set up the hyper-gravitational repelling force field at the approach of any ship to the planet's surface – regardless whether they knew the coded password or not for the eventuality that previous events had taken place which were regarded as suspicious and hazardous by the positronic brain.

This emergency had arisen the moment the brain had shot down the two destroyers. Although they definitely belonged to Rhodan's fleet, nevertheless they did not know the secret code signal. And despite the fact that the *Good Hope* was also one of Rhodan's ships, and even had known the secret signal, it had already been too late. The repelling field had already been erected and could only be removed by some special manipulation inside the station.

No one but an Arkonide or Rhodan himself could penetrate into the fortress, because they were the only persons with a special unique brain pattern which was a prerequisite for admittance to the Base.

An impasse had been reached which only Thora or Rhodan, but never Bell, would be able to overcome.

It was fortunate at this moment that Bell had no inkling of this arrangement. His rage against the positronic brain would have known no limits.

The spacesphere kept circling the planet constantly at the same altitude. It was unable to descend any lower because of the invisible protective energy screen. Bell and his crew could not recognize anything on the planet's surface; even their instruments failed to penetrate the dense cloud layer. Suriu Wengu was the sole exception. As a mutant 'seer' he could peer through the cloud envelope to the planet's surface. His special gift permitted him to see through solid matter. He could recognize the jungles, swamps, oceans and mountains but this was not of much help to Bell in his present predicament.

'I am convinced something happened to Rhodan. If it turns out that the positronic brain is to blame for any mishap, I'll make personally sure to take it apart piece by piece and grind it to metal dust!'

Ralf Marten was skeptical. 'That's a bit premature because absolutely nobody can land on Venus now. The planet is totally isolated. I do not know what has taken place but I am positive that the station's automatic installations could not be blamed for any malfunction, they are 100% reliable. No power in the universe could hinder them in the discharge of their duties.'

'Duties!' shrieked Bell, unnerved. 'What does this silly tin can understand about duties? It would be its duty to help us and Perry Rhodan. Instead . . . pooh!' He turned away to call Seiko in the radio center. 'Keep calling and try to establish contact with Rhodan! He must be somewhere down there – somewhere in those jungles and swamps with all those prehistoric monsters.'

He emitted a sigh and let himself fall back into his pilot's seat to brood over his somber thoughts and doleful conjectures.

Meanwhile the veiled planet kept slowly rotating below the spacesphere – a planet that refused to yield its secret.

Dawn broke while they were still descending from the rocky plateau.

Far over to the East, Rhodan sighted a delicate, faint lightness in the impenetrable darkness. The first pastel-pink arrows shot across the horizon and tinted the uppermost cloud layers. Very slowly, the light began to filter through, and it took hours before there was some idea where the sun actually was.

But it was not yet so far.

Okura had led them safely and warned them on any obstacle in their path. There was no sign that they were being followed and it was most likely several hours before their flight would be noticed.

This suited Perry Rhodan perfectly. He had no intention of mixing in the fight among the scattered units of the invasion troops whom he regarded secretly as the first settlers on Venus. Still he would warn Gen Tomisenkow in any case, if he ever reached him. There was some doubt in his mind that he actually would get that far.

Stretched out between the two plateaus lay the lowlands with their treacherous swamps. Rabow explained it would be more dangerous to cross the swamps by day than by night, for the giant saurian lizards would soon awake and wander about in search of food. They were mainly vegetarians, which however did not prevent them from attacking any animals or human beings in whom they recognized undesirable competitors and trespassers in their domain.

The men relied on their absolutely dependable ray-guns and reassured Rabow, who felt rather helpless with his pistol in case they were confronted by one of the original inhabitants of the jungle world. There was no need to worry about food, they had sufficient provisions until they would arrive at Tomisenkow's camp, which should not take any longer than 20 hours at most. Their water supply could easily be replenished at the river.

When they reached the spot where they had been surprised by Rabow, it was light enough to recognize details of the surrounding area. The sight was none too pleasant.

The waterfall soon became a swift flowing river which

in turn emptied into a large lake. Their path – explained Rabow – was meandering through the grass land along its shores. The jungle growth would occasionally come right up to the very edge of the lake. Fog rose from the steamy surface of the water, blending with the low-lying cloud banks. The sun was now visible in the East, a faded reddish stain in the haze.

Life began to stir in the lake. Whirlpools became visible in spots, then the giant bodies of various types of saurians broke through the surface of the water. The monsters generally resembled their prehistoric cousins that once upon a time had lived on Earth. Some animals remained in the shallow waters off shore and started to graze underwater in the vegetation. These were the less dangerous types.

Others swam and waded ashore, swaying clumsily across the grassy strip lining the shore and then disappeared in the jungle. They left behind a wide path of devastated land as they would leisurely stop to uproot and devour small trees.

Rhodan watched the scene with great interest. 'What a wonderful opportunity for you, Marshall, to find out what and if these monsters really are thinking. Do you believe their brains can send out thought streams like the higher life forms?'

'It would not surprise me,' replied the telepath pensively. 'Their thoughts might not be much to speak of but it would be presumptuous on our part to deny they might be capable of cerebral activity. All living creatures think, even an ant. Only man assumes himself to be exclusively endowed with the ability to think. That distinguishes him from animals but certainly not in a positive sense. But we who are traveling through space are different than our earthbound fellow men. We have encountered alien races and realize that intelligence has nothing to do with external appearances. Therefore we have rid ourselves of prejudices inasfar as we ever had any. We know that the ruling race of a planet might look like lizards – and this brought forth in us genuine respect for the animals of our own world. We can no longer regard a dog as a mere animal, we look upon him as a life form that distinguishes itself from the human race only because it is thinking in a different manner than we do.'

'Do you see a relationship in our ability to appreciate extraterrestrial races on the one hand and our love for our own animals on the other hand?' wondered Rhodan, although the connection began to dawn on him.

'Very definitely so,' answered Marshall with conviction. 'I will even go as far as to say that only the true animal lover is properly suited to forge ahead into space and make contact with the inhabitants of other planets. He alone shows the necessary understanding and will not shy away from giving recognition to the most impossible life forms as being worthy of enjoying equal rights. This fact, some day, might spell the difference between peace and war in the entire universe.'

Rhodan did not reply. He looked down into the steaming jungle plain of the primeval world. He realized that they looked just like the plains on Earth millions of years ago. At that time animals had ruled as masters over the whole planet, for man had made his appearance only much later. Man owed his existence to the animals, just as the animals owed theirs to the plants. One followed the other, one had taken over from the other; and all were interdependent. One could not survive without the other.

And yet all lived from fighting each other – by eating and being eaten . . .

Rhodan pulled himself together. 'We'll make it alright. Even the mightiest giants are vulnerable when it comes to our pulse-ray guns. Nevertheless I hope we won't be forced to kill too many of them. This world belongs to them and they belong in it. Let's go!'

Sgt Rabow marched in the lead, followed by Rhodan. Marshall and Okura brought up the rear. It was not long before they arrived at the large swamp lake. Rabow remained at a certain distance from the water; he wanted to stay as far away from the damp shore as possible. The soil under the huge trees was still relatively dry and and encounter here with one of the saurians seemed most unlikely.

Everything went along fine until they had rounded the last bay and left the lake behind. All that still separated them from Tomisenkow's encampment was a three-mile-wide stretch of grass land. The grass grew to a height of 12 to 15 feet. It effectively blocked the men's view. The ground became increasingly moist and resilient. They felt like they were walking on a giant sponge and they had lost the sensation of relative security they had earlier experienced in the jungle.

Rabow pointed toward their destination. It loomed up like a dark-colored island from the ocean of white-violet water-saturated cloud formations. 'Here is the path we usually have been following – but only at night. The ground will get drier from now on.'

He speeded up his steps in order to place the danger zone behind them as fast as he could. Rhodan followed close behind him, holding his raygun ready to shoot.

Suddenly Rabow uttered a shrill scream, drew his pistol and emptied the whole magazine into an expanse of grass land directly in front of them. Then he jumped back and bumped into Rhodan so violently that he almost lost his balance.

Okura stretched out his arm and pointed forward where the high grass suddenly parted. Rhodan felt his heart stand still as he saw the monster creeping toward them, totally ignoring the bullet hail which bounced harmlessy off its hide. It measured nearly 30 feet in length, resembled the legendary dragons of our ancestors. It walked on four legs. On its back rose a toothed crest made of a tough horny substance. Its eyes were winking maliciously in its smallish head. Tufts of grass and tree roots were dangling from its wide lizard snout.

'A stegosaurus,' Rhodan said in awe. 'It's supposed to be a harmless vegetarian. If only we weren't blocking its path now . . .'

'Shoot it *please!*' begged Rabow, trembling all over. 'It will trample us all to a fine mush in a moment. They will attack men – I have seen it happen many a time here.'

Marshall stepped over to one side and took aim. Rhodan looked at him disapprovingly and shook his head. 'Wait, Marshall!'

Okura seemed to know instinctively that Rhodan wanted to gain time for some experiment despite the precariousness of their situation. He, too, moved off the wide path and waited on a small island of grass. Rhodan nodded his head almost imperceptibly without taking his eyes of the stegosaurus.

The enormous animal dragged its heavy body through the grass, all the while coming closer and closer. Its swift eyes followed the movements of the men but it made no preparations to follow them. Rhodan seized Rabow by the hand and pulled him off the road. Eventually, the saurian passed by a few yards away without paying any attention to them. It rolled like a bulldozer over the vegetation, leaving behind a regular four-to-five yard wide road which traversed the primeval prairie. A powerful temblor seemed to shake the ground whenever the monster's armored tail thumped on it. Soon the stegosaurus began to browse peacefully.

Rhodan turned to Marshall with a triumphant smile and noticed his baffled expression.

'It was thinking,' mumbled Marshall, still beside himself. 'It was actually thinking!'

'What was it thinking about?'

'It was thinking so clearly that I could have sworn it was a human being passing by.'

'What's the matter? Did that monster get your tongue?'

'It was thinking: "Would it be worth my while stomping that bothersome vermin into the ground?"'

'Vermin?' said Okura full of doubt.

Marshall insisted: 'Yes, it was thinking of vermin, and it meant us by that.'

Rhodan grinned slightly. 'Not very flattering for us but it reinforces the theory which we had just been discussing. That's something, I must admit. But, enough of that, we have no time to waste. Anyhow, I am glad we were not forced to kill it. It had clear thoughts and it deserves to live.'

They followed the trampled-down track of the stegosaurus for a short stretch, then Rabow made a right turn. He had not understood a single word of the conversation and must have thought his three companions to be totally off their rockers but he refrained from asking any questions.

Soon they arrived at the steep rock wall and started to ascend. They followed a well-worn footpath and reached the edge of the plateau after a two hours' climb.

Rabow peered around cautiously but did not seem to find what he was looking for. 'The sentries,' he said to Rhodan and sounded quite confused. 'They aren't here. That's strange. There have always been two men standing here.'

'How far is it to Tomisenkow's camp?' asked Rhodan. He had put his raygun back in his holster.

'About 10 minutes, not more.'

'Let's go then!'

The fact that the sentries were missing upset Rabow considerably. He could not figure out why Tomisenkow's vigilance should have relaxed all of a sudden. Wasn't the General normally the embodiment of suspicion?

'Over there, beyond those boulders, are the first huts,' began Rabow, but before he could complete his sentence all hell broke loose.

At the onset of a shrill howling whine, Rhodan and his two companions dropped instantaneously to the ground. Unfortunately, Rabow's reactions were much slower. He was still standing upright when he caught the full blast of the machinegun fire coming from some low bushes. He staggered a couple of steps forward, halted and finally sank slowly to the ground.

Rhodan realized that from this moment on they were without a guide. They would have to find the way to Thora unaided. But he also knew something else. . .

A violent pain coursed through his right shoulder; it felt as if someone had thrust a burning hot iron into his flesh. He must have stopped a bullet as he threw himself onto the ground.

Gen Tomisenkow seems to have concentrated his troops in the village, thought Rhodan, and then have activated an automatically functioning defense perimeter. This way nobody could approach the village; they would be gunned down by hidden machine gun emplacements if they came too close.

Marshall knew at once what had happened. Despite the hail of bullets he leapt to Rhodan's side and examined him. 'It's only a flesh wound. We've got to get out of here! Okura, give me a hand!'

Rhodan moaned with pain but he still managed to co-operate with Marshall and Okura as they dragged him back a few yards. As if by a miracle, the infernal rat-a-tat-tat of the concealed machinegun nests ceased abruptly. They had moved outside the barrier zone.

Rabow was beyond help: he was dead. At least he was spared now having to make the painful decision between Tomisenkow and Wallerinski.

The two men were relieved when Rhodan declared that he was able to walk now after the initial shock had worn off. They walked on either side of him and endeavored to put as much space as possible between themselves and the deathtrap surrounding the village. Not even their pulse-ray guns could be of any help here where they could not sight their target.

Way to the rear they heard the shouting of commands. Some men called out; an occasional shot was being fired. Silence fell again.

'Will we stay on here on the plateau?' Marshall wanted to know.

Rhodan tried to ignore the hurt in his right shoulder. 'Over there to the right are more trees; we'll find some temporary shelter there. Marshall, can't you find out what the men plan to do? They aren't too far away from us?'

'Let's wait a while, I need more quiet to concentrate properly,' said Marshall. 'First things first. We must get you to a safe place and take care of your wound.'

Rhodan did not argue. He knew he could rely on his friends, and besides, he felt the need to preserve his strength.

They penetrated a short stretch into the relatively sparse jungle growth and eventually located a gigantic tree which was completely enveloped by a network of creeper plants. It was easy to climb and even Rhodan needed very little assistance. He could manage by pulling himself up with his left hand a little stretch at a time.

Twenty yards above the ground they reached a suitable spot. A broad, flattened tree trunk lay across several trees, supported by the tangle of their thick branches. A curtain of primeval lianas afforded protectiton in all directions. They had found here a natural tree house whose walls could later be reinforced by branches and large leaves.

Rhodan's wound was not serious; the bullet had passed clean through the shoulder muscle. Marshall applied a bandage and gave Rhodan an anti-fever pill. Hardly 10 minutes later, the wounded man had fallen asleep, and his regular breathing promised that he would soon be well again. Okura and Marshall could not sleep, they were too restless after the past events.

'We are stuck here,' whispered Okura softly, since he did not wish to disturb Rhodan's slumber. 'Thora is in Tomisenkow's hands and we are squatting on this jungle tree like helpless monkeys, waiting for some miracle. Goodness knows where Bell might be. He is taking his time; after all, he hasn't the faintest idea what bad luck we've had on Venus. But, anyhow, it's about time that he starts worrying.'

Okura had, of course, no way of knowing that Bell was orbiting Venus high above them in the *Good Hope V* and that he, too, was waiting for a miracle that would permit him to come in for a landing on this infernal planet. Their radio station was constantly trying to establish communication with anybody down there on Venus. But their receiver remained consistently silent.

Marshall rummaged disconsolately through their meager provisions. 'That will keep us going only for a short while,' he concluded his examination. 'We'll have to go hunting for more food.'

'It will take at least three to four days before Rhodan can properly use his arm again. We should stay at least that long in this shelter here.'

'That makes sense,' said Marshall; 'let's get some rest at least. I want to sleep. Will you keep watch?'

'Who else?' grinned Okura and settled as comfortably as possible on his branch, leaning his back against the thick main tree trunk. His pulse-ray gun lay across his knees, ready to shoot instantly if needed.

Several hours of sound sleep and a hearty meal restored Rhodan's usual vigor. His wound healed thanks to the excellent medications which had also suppressed any infection and fever.

They were discussing their situation and various plans for further action. 'Trying to establish contact with Tomisenkow is out of question,' summarized Rhodan after they had considered the pros and cons of divers points. 'He is guarding Thora like a priceless treasure and will make his demands on his own terms, eventually. There is no news from Bell. He ought to have landed by now at the station – unless the robot brain has activated the secret barrier X that I myself programmed into it. That, of course, would mean that Bell cannot land here; and even more: not a living soul can land on Venus!'

'How can we get out of here? Who will rescue us?' worried Okura.

'There is only one chance, and that is for me to reach the fortress on foot and reprogram the positronic brain. But that is not the most urgent task at hand. I want to free Thora first from Tomisenkow's hands.'

'Didn't you say just now . . . ?' began Marshall, but then fell silent. He seemed to have pried in Rhodan's thoughts. 'I almost forgot them,' he concluded after a moment.

Okura looked from one to the other; he was baffled. Since he was unable to read thoughts he could not know what Marshall was referring to. Rhodan came to his assistance. 'Many years ago, when we first landed on this planet, we encountered half-intelligent seal-like creatures at the shores of the primeval ocean. Our telepaths could communicate with them and we got along fine. On one occasion I even helped them out by doing them a favor. Perhaps they have not forgotten that and are willing to return the favor now. It would not make any sense if the three of us would start out on the long trek to the primeval ocean, which must be located somewhere east of here. And only a telepath can communicate with the seals and explain what it is that we want from them. We'll discuss the details later on but I hardly believe we could find any better solution to our problem.'

'A telepath!' moaned Marshall. 'That means me! All alone through the jungle!' He fingered his wide wristband which harbored a variety of tiny instruments. 'Shouldn't we rather try again to establish contact with Bell?'

'Sure, we'll do that, too, but if SBX has gone into effect, getting in touch with Bell won't be of any help to us. The seal creatures know the way to the fortress; they can lead us there. No, Marshall, I'm afraid you're stuck with this job. Okura and I will wait here for you. And in case something new should develop in respect to Tomisenkow, I'll leave a message for you.'

'And our provisions? What'll we live on?'

'You have your pistol and we can hunt for food,' Rhodan reassured him. 'We can try it with our pulse-ray gun.'

'That won't be necessary,' remarked Okura and pulled a heavy pistol from his belt. 'There was no point,' he apologized, 'in letting Rabow's weapon fall into the hands of Tomisenkow's men. We can get more meat with that than we can possibly eat.'

'Now that everything is taken care of, Marshall, you'd better catch a few more hours' sleep. Later we'll discuss further details about your trip.'

Meanwhile it had become day. The bright daylight pierced the canopy of the jungle and removed the last vestiges of the all-concealing veils of the night. The tree house seemed to swim in a sea of bright orchids which floated like giant jelly-fish in a green ocean. Multi-colored bugs were crawling and scurrying over the branches and the tree trunks. From higher up came a cacaphony of cawing, twittering and singing, contributed to the riot of color and sound by the feathered inhabitants of the primeval jungle.

Marshall had taken leave of Rhodan and Okura and had climbed down to the jungle floor. There he paused for a moment, heavy-hearted, feeling lost among the giant trees, and waved a last farewell to his friends. Then he resolutely set out on his march toward the washed-out spot of the sun that stood somewhere far to the east above the green wilderness. A few minutes later he had disappeared from sight, swallowed by the dense underbrush. For a little while longer, Rhodan and Okura could still hear his cautiously advancing steps; then they, too, vanished.

Rhodan and Okura remained alone in their tree house. They were condemned to inactivity until Marshall's return. That might take several days. Bright daylight would last another 120 hours before once more the long Venusian night would fall. If Marshall could accomplish his mission by then, they would have made a giant step forward. However, if not . . .

Okura sat lost in somber thoughts, idly fingering his all-purpose instrument, worn like a wristband, when suddenly a hardly audible voice came from the miniaturized loudspeaker:

'. . . calling Perry Rhodan! We're calling Perry Rhodan! Come in, Perry Rhodan!'

The voice grew louder, as if the sender were approaching rapidly, broadcasting the same message over and over again.

Okura switched on the direction finder immediately and then looked almost straight up. His features expressed doubt. Rhodan smiled: 'That's Bell. Send the signal!'

Several seconds later they could clearly hear Bell's voice call out in astonishment which soon changed to relief: 'Perry, Perry, where the devil are you hiding yourself? I've been searching for you like a needle in a haystack. Why the long radio silence?'

'Take it easy, Reg. Where are you calling from?'

'From the *Good Hope V*; we are circling above this damned planet and can't come in for a landing. That cursed positronic brain . . .'

'So, that's it!' Rhodan interrupted and sighed. 'Now it's certain that nobody is able to land on Venus. Bell, you'd better return to Earth and wait for a message from me that I have arrived at the station. There's nothing else you can do for me now.'

'Where's Thora?'

'She's in good hands,' replied Rhodan sarcastically.

'I'm not returning to Earth,' said Bell suddenly. His voice sounded rather faint already, because of the increasing distance. 'I'm going to stay here until I'm able to land. And that's all there is to it!'

Rhodan knew his friend well enough to recognize this special tone of voice. Nothing in the universe would now deter Bell from what he had decided to do.

'Alright, then, just keep on orbiting Venus. Okura and I are perched on a tree in the jungle, playing Tarzan, while Marshall is on his way to negotiate with the Venusian seals. Otherwise, everything is just fine down here. Say hello to everyone on the *Good Hope V*!'

Bell's voice was almost inaudible by now but Okura could have sworn his reply had been a hearty curse.

Rhodan smiled, trying to hide the pain in his shoulder. He leaned back against the curtain formed by huge lianas. A blood-red orchid, as big as a man's head, hung just above his head. 'He'll be cursing more than once, if I know him!

115

He hates nothing worse than having to stand idly by while others enjoy all kinds of adventures.'

'And he can't even join in all the fun second hand and watch it from up there,' joked Okura, pointing to the eternal cloud layer above the jungle canopy.

Rhodan closed his eyes and nodded, saying nothing. There was so much to be done, so many gigantic tasks to be undertaken. His life's work had just begun; he had no more than laid a foundation stone. Somewhere far away in the Milky Way the star realm of the Arkonides was crumbling away and decaying. Perhaps at this very moment new invasion fleets were taking off, light years away, planning to pay Earth a surprise visit.

For the time being, fate had wrested responsibility from his hands, but he was certain it would be returned to him some day, increased a thousand fold.

And while the giant saurians were browsing in the grassy lowlands, making their way back to the ocean through the swampy shores, stomping and roaring; while Thora was doggedly bargaining for her price with Gen Tomisenkow; while Marshall was making his way all alone through the desolate jungle; and while Bell continued to orbit in helpless rage around and around the planet – Perry Rhodan slept peacefully on Venus, recuperating his strength.

Son Okura watched faithfully over his leader, making certain nothing disturbed the Peacelord's sleep.

The future was used to waiting for the present to catch up with it. The hour of decision had been moved far ahead and the future waited patiently for tomorrow and tomorrow ... and Perry Rhodan.

A MIDSUMMER TEMPEST

Poul Anderson

'The best writing he's done in years ... his language is superb. Worth buying for your permanent collection.'

– *The Alien Critic*

Somewhere, spinning through another universe, is an Earth where a twist of fate, a revolution and a few early inventions have made a world quite unlike our own.

It is a world where Cavaliers and Puritans battle with the aid of observation balloons and steam trains; where Oberon and Titania join forces with King Arthur to resist the Industrial Revolution; and where the future meshes with the past in the shape of Valeria, time traveller from New York.

PROTECTOR

Larry Niven

Phssthpok the Pak had been travelling for most of his 32,000 years – his mission, to save, develop and protect the group of pak breeders sent out into space some 2½ million years before . . .

Brennan was a Belter, the product of a fiercely independent, somewhat anarchic society living in, on and around an outer asteroid belt. The Belters were rebels one and all, and Brennan was a Smuggler. The Belt worlds had been tracking the pak ship for days – Brennan figured to meet that ship first . . .

He was never seen again – at least not in the form of homo sapiens.

Larry Niven is the author of RINGWORLD which won both the Hugo and Nebula awards for the best s.f. novel of the year.

THE FLIGHT OF THE HORSE

Larry Niven

These are the stories of Svetz the harassed Time Retrieval Expert and of the mind-bending difficulties created when his Department supplies him with inadequate information. . . .

Here too are his strange adventures with horses, unicorns, ostriches, rocs and other unlikely fauna, both extinct and as yet unborn . . . In THE FLIGHT OF THE HORSE, Larry Niven has written a collection of science fiction stories which combine fantasy and mainstream s.f. with superb story telling.

BEFORE THE GOLDEN AGE 1

Isaac Asimov

For many s.f. addicts the Golden Age began in 1938 when John Campbell became editor of Astounding Stories. For Isaac Asimov, the formative and most memorable period came in the decade before the Golden Age – the 1930s. It is to the writers of this generation that BEFORE THE GOLDEN AGE is dedicated.

Some – Jack Williamson, Murray Leinster, Stanley Weinbaum and Asimov himself – have remained famous to this day. Others such as Neil Jones, S. P. Meek and Charles Tanner, have been deservedly rescued from oblivion.

BEFORE THE GOLDEN AGE was originally published in the United States in a single mammoth volume of almost 1,200 pages. The British paperback edition will appear in four books, the first of which covers the years 1930 to 1933.